Alien Feeling

The Magical Midlife Series
By
Rose Bak

Table of Contents

Copyright

---

1.   https://paperorpixels.com/

About This Book

Living in a town full of shifters, witches, vampires, and other mystical creatures, she thinks she's seen everything. She was wrong.

Marian

When I was offered the job as head librarian in a small town in Colorado, I was thrilled. (Yeah, yeah, I'm a librarian named Marian, cue the musical jokes.) Sure, I'm one of the only humans in this magical little part of the world, but the residents welcome me with open arms.

At least I thought they did, before someone tried to play an April Fool's joke on me. There's no way the hot younger guy flirting with me is into a middle-aged woman like me. Oh, and the fake blue skin is taking the joke a little too far...but I can't help but wish this was real. Also, why am I suddenly having prophetic dreams since this guy showed up?

Edfollopxen (or Ed, to his new friends)

When I left my home planet of Genervia in search of my fated mate, I had no idea I'd find one as perfect as the curvy little human they call Marian on the very first planet I visited. It may take a while to win her love, but I'm willing to put in the work. I'm reading about her culture, getting a job with the wolves, and making it my mission to keep her so satisfied that she forgets how different we really are.

Can a grouchy librarian and a cheerfully naive alien really find love?

Alien Feeling is a steamy midlife paranormal romantic comedy featuring a woman with burgeoning psychic skills who doesn't believe in fated mates, a big blue alien who doesn't believe in personal space, and a town full of nosy matchmakers determined to help them find their happily ever after.

About the "Magical Midlife" series: Just outside the shifter town of Greysden sits Rosewater Manor, a place shrouded in magic. The

Rosewater women and their friends all have special gifts, although sometimes they're a bit glitchy. At least until they find true love...

Join My Mailing List

Join Rose Bak's mailing list at bit.ly/RoseBakNewsletter[2]. You'll get a free book and be the first to hear about all the latest releases and special sales.

2. https://d.docs.live.net/ae511949052ccd53/Documents/bit.ly/RoseBakNewsletter

Dedication

For every woman who's every felt frumpy, unattractive and/or unloved.
Hopefully, there's a hot alien coming for you.

Marian

"Hey, Marian the Librarian, how are you doing?"

I rolled my eyes as my friend Pepper walked into the library. That's right, my name was Marian and I worked in Library Sciences. If I had a dollar for every idiot that sung about seventy-six trombones or the Wells Fargo wagon when they met me, I'd be a retired librarian right now.

Of course if I were a retired librarian, I'd probably still be a volunteer here, because I loved working in the library. It wasn't just about the books. It was about creating a community of learning and knowledge. Librarians were society's secret guardians of free thought, and I loved that.

When the job as head librarian of the Greysden Library came up, I'd jumped at the chance despite Greysden's reputation of being a little different. Turns out "different" meant that the town was primarily home to shifters and other magical creatures, like my friend Pepper.

"How's it going Pepper?" I greeted her.

I'd only been in Greysden for about a year and a half, but Pepper was already one of my best friends. The daughter of a witch and a psychic, she'd gone through her whole life thinking she had no magical powers until last Halloween when it came out that her aunt had accidentally performed a magic suppression spell on her. She'd spent the last few months trying to bring forth her witchy powers, with only limited success. She was currently enrolled in Witchcraft 101 class with a bunch of grade schoolers.

"I'm doing okay. I'm looking for a new romantic comedy series. I finished all of Lucy Score's latest series and now I need something to tide me over while I'm waiting for her next book."

"Sure, I've got some suggestions for books you might like."

We were walking towards the romantic fiction section when I heard the main door open. I looked up automatically. And up...

The guy who came in was tall, at least six and a half feet tall, maybe more. He was broad, with wide shoulders, huge biceps, legs like freaking tree trunks, and washboard abs that were visible beneath the thin fabric of the jumpsuit he wore.

Jumpsuit? *It figures,* I thought, *all the good looking guys are gay – or already mated.*

The guy looked a little blue. And not depressed. Blue like his skin was blue. What kind of shifter turned blue? I wondered. After living in Greysden for a while I thought I'd seen everything by now, but maybe not.

My eyes rose to his handsome face. He had dark eyes that were almost black, a strong jaw, ears that were the slightest bit pointy, and sharp cheekbones. He was beautiful. And young. He looked like he was in his twenties, much younger than my forty-five. Not that I could have gotten a guy that hot when I was younger anyway.

"Can I help you?" I asked, hoping I wasn't drooling.

His head whipped around at the sound of my voice. When our eyes met, I felt the oddest sense of, I didn't know how to describe it, but it was almost like there was a jolt and then some invisible string joined us together. I had to stop myself from running towards him like he'd just returned from war.

The guy reared back like someone had smacked him.

"My soul mate," he whispered, his voice sounding awed. "I found you!"

"Again?"

Pepper's irritated voice broke my reverie, and I turned to look at her questioningly.

"What?" I asked.

"I can't believe this is happening again. I should just rent myself out as a mate finder," she grumbled. "Maybe that's my magical ability after all. Not that I can find my own damn mate. No, I'm destined to be all alone while everyone around me finds love."

"Pepper!" I raised my voice a bit to break through her ranting. "What are you talking about?"

She nodded to where the big blue guy was still staring at me in shock.

"Hey buddy, did you say that Marian here is your soulmate?"

The guy nodded. "Yes, she is my true mate. My soul recognizes her as my destiny."

I ignored the shiver of pleasure I felt at that proclamation. Then I remembered the date.

"Oh I get it, this is some kind of April Fool's Day joke, right? Mess with the frumpy middle-aged librarian?" I asked.

The guy frowned in confusion. "What is this 'April Fool's Day', my mate?"

"You're not frumpy," Pepper said at the same time. She was a good friend, despite the musical jokes.

"What kind of shifter are you anyway, big guy?" I asked, ignoring them both.

When the blue man just looked at me in confusion, I turned to Pepper, who shook her head.

"I've lived here all my life and never saw a blue shifter before. I don't even know if there are any animals in nature that are blue. At least not that shade of blue."

"Shifter?" the guy said, looking upwards like he was querying something in his own brain. "Do you refer to the creatures called shapeshifters, the ones who are part human and part animal?"

"Got it in one, Blue Man Group," I quipped.

"I am not a shapeshifter. I come to you from the planet Genervia."

I burst out laughing. "Sure you do, Blue Man Group."

"My name is Edfollopxen." His voice was deep and made me feel kind of tingly.

"Edfollopxen?" I asked.

"Edfollopxen," he corrected, emphasizing the middle syllables.

"Edfollopxen," I tried again.

"No, Edfollopxen," he repeated.

"That's a mouthful, so how about I just call you Ed?" I suggested.

"Ed? This is a…" he paused, once again looking upwards towards his brain, "nickname, a diminutive that humans give to their friends and loved ones?"

"Yep."

"Ed is acceptable to me then," he said almost formally. He had a strange way of speaking although he had no accent.

"Awesome. Now if you're done messing with me, Ed, I have an actual job to do here," I said. "What do you need from the library?"

"You."

I huffed in frustration. Some people didn't know when to give up on a joke.

"Yeah, okay then, I'll let you see yourself out. Goodbye."

Edfollopxen

I watched my soulmate turn away, her curvy hips taunting me as she strode away from me. It made both of my hearts pinch in my chest.

She was the most beautiful woman I'd ever seen, here or on any planet. She was quite small, several hands width shorter than me, but lush and womanly, with rounded hips, a soft belly, and full breasts that I longed to get my hands on.

Marian had a heart shaped face that was the most unusual shade, a very pale beige like the color of an Earth drink I'd tried yesterday called "latte". Her eyes were large and brown, with interesting little lines at the outside corners. Her delectable mouth was the color of my favorite plant back home on Genervia, a cross between dark pink and light red, with more fine lines that appeared when she pursed her lips at me in displeasure.

I wasn't sure what I'd done to annoy her, but I was immediately determined to correct my error.

I'd left Genervia in search of my soulmate. Everyone on my planet mated for life, and if it became clear that our soulmates did not reside on our planet, it was our practice to travel to other planets with compatible females to try our luck there.

Luck was on my side for sure – Earth was the first planet I'd visited in my search and here she was, my sweet little soulmate.

I'd landed in the woods outside of a place called Greysden, Colorado. It was a very beautiful place, very lush and green, not dissimilar from parts of Genervia. I'd walked around town exploring yesterday and when I told the bear man who worked at the coffee shop that I sought more knowledge about this world, he'd suggested a place called the "library".

When I walked into the library I'd immediately felt something different. Every part of my body had tingled in excitement to such an extent that I'd initially frozen in place, unable to move until I heard my soulmate's voice asking if she could help me. When my eyes met with the beautiful human female, I knew I'd finally found the other half of my soul.

I just needed to get her, as the humans said, on the same page as me.

"Wait," I called out. "What is your name, female?"

She turned around and gave me a frown I did not understand.

"Marian. And I swear to God if you make any Music Man jokes, you're out of here."

"I will not make Music Man jokes," I promised solemnly, adding this to my mental list of things I must research about Earth. Whatever a Music Man joke was, my soulmate did not like it, so I must avoid this.

"If you please Marian, I am seeking books about Earth culture."

Another frown, followed by a sigh. "Right this way."

I followed her through the large building which was filled with rows of what I knew were books. On my home planet, only the most ancient tomes were printed on paper, everything else was available on our communication tablets.

My mate walked quickly, but I easily kept up with her, my eyes fixed to the round muscles of her curvy ass flexing beneath her skirt. I couldn't wait to get my hands on her, but I knew I needed to proceed with caution. I'd heard from other Genervians who'd come to Earth that sometimes the women needed some time to accept their soulmate status.

Marian pointed to one of the shelves. "What you're looking for is right here."

Grabbing the entire row of books, I nodded my appreciation.

"Thank you, Marian. I will read these and endeavor to learn your ways so I may please you as a mate."

As I walked away she called, "Wait, are you taking all of those? You know you have to bring them back, right?"

"I will bring them back to you in one rotation of your sun," I reassured her. "Then we must talk about our mating."

Her mouth dropped open and for some reason I had a very naughty image of filling it with my *afgha*, as we called it in the Genervian language.

"Until tomorrow, sweet Marian."

I hurried back to my ship, eager to read all I could about Earth now that I knew it would be my new home. Genervia was a matriarchal society, so it was typical for the male to move in with the female.

After I'd gotten settled on Earth and our initial mating frenzy was complete, I would take Marian back to Genervia for a visit. My parents would be eager to meet her. Although they might be interested in visiting Earth instead, I'd have to consult with them.

For the next few hours I skimmed through the books Marian recommended, making notes on my comms, which served as both a communication device and repository for information. It had access to the Earth internet, but their internet was filled with so many different things I struggled to find the information I wanted.

I didn't understand the Earth fascination with videos featuring the creatures they called "cats" or the platforms that were filled with pictures of people's meals.

With the help of the library books, I was able to dig in more and search their internet more effectively. I researched Earth customs and manners, how I should dress on this planet, and learned more about the human animal "shapeshifters" that lived here in Greysden.

I also searched for "Music Man jokes" but I only found something the humans called "memes", pictures with words on them that just left me more confused about Marian's warning.

When I'd soaked up as much information about Earth culture as I could, I researched how to please a human woman. As was customary in my world, I had saved my body for my soulmate. No female of any species had touched my *afgha*, but I was eager to take that step with Marian. I'd been half hard since I'd first heard her voice.

By the time I finished my research, many hours had passed and the Earth's single moon was high in the night sky. I fell into an exhausted sleep and my last thought before I succumbed to slumber was about my soulmate.

Marian

I'd spent a restless night obsessing about the weird blue guy from the library yesterday. I wanted to be skeptical about him saying he was from another planet, but honestly after spending a year in Greysden, I'd learned that there were many different forms of sentient life besides humans.

It wasn't that humans didn't know that shifters, witches, fae and other magical creatures existed, it was more that they pretended to be the only inhabitants of the planet. It was easier that way. When I'd moved to Greysden I'd been a little surprised that shifters weren't a myth, but now that I knew some of them, I realized they were just like us. Except for the turning into animals part of course.

Another thing about shifters: they had good genes. Every damned shifter I'd met had been fit and attractive, and the rest of the magical creatures weren't exactly ugly either. But none of them held a candle to Edfoll—, um, Ed. He looked like some CGI version of a hot alien.

I couldn't help but be attracted to him. After all, I was a red-blooded heterosexual woman with eyes and a pulse. But he was young, and I was middle aged. He was the best looking guy I'd ever seen in real life and I was, well, average at best.

Plus, I was sure he was fucking with me. Despite Pepper's insistence that she'd seen people find their mates multiple times and it was always just like what had transpired between me and Ed, I didn't believe for a minute the alien was serious.

If he really was from another planet, he had to be a superior life form if his people had mastered personal space travel. No superior life form was going to be interested in a middle-aged small town librarian.

Every time the door opened at work my eyes flew to see who it was. I was on edge all day, despite telling myself that Ed had likely absconded with my books and would never be seen again.

Imagine my surprise when he strolled in just around two o'clock, holding two coffees. When he saw me, his face broke out in a smile, showing incisors that were a bit longer and pointy, like fangs. Instead of his jumpsuit he was wearing jeans and a plain black tee shirt that hugged him like a second skin.

"Soulmate Marian," he said smoothly. "I have conferred with the bear man at the coffee establishment, and he assured me that you have a fondness for something called a vanilla latte."

He handed me a cup, and I inhaled the sweet smell of my favorite coffee drink.

"Bear man? You mean Charlie?" I asked, referencing the cheerful bear shifter who ran Bearly Beans, our local coffee shop.

"Yes, Charlie, the man who is also a bear." He tapped on the side of his nose. "Genervians have a very good sense of smell."

God, I hope that didn't mean he could smell the way I'd gotten aroused the second he showed up.

"Well thanks for the coffee," I said, reaching to take the cup from his hand.

I closed my eyes and took a long sip, sighing happily as the mixture of coffee, milk, and vanilla hit my tongue. When I opened my eyes, Ed was staring at me with the oddest expression on his face. He looked almost...hungry.

"Are you here for more books?" I asked. "Because I really need you to return the ones you already have before you take more. You're already over the limit."

"No, I am not here for books. I am here to see you and talk about our mating."

"That joke is getting old, Ed. April's Fool's Day is over and I'm trying to work here. I don't have time for nonsense."

"Our mating is not a joke." His expression was earnest. "I looked up that word last night and learned that it means to say something to cause amusement in another. I don't want to amuse you, Marian, I want to mate with you. You are the other half of my soul, and my body aches for you."

For just an instant, I felt a thrill. Then I got angry. Setting my coffee on the counter, I stalked closer and poked him in the chest with my finger. It was like poking a rock.

I'd intended to chastise him, but then Ed grabbed my hand in his, his larger hand engulfing my much smaller one. I caught my breath as an arousal stronger than anything I'd ever felt slammed into me like a kick to the head. My eyes flew up to meet his, and as we stared at each other I felt the oddest sensation.

It seemed impossible, but there was some kind of localized vibration coming from his hands even though his body was still. The vibration headed up my arm and traveled right to my core. Holding his hand was like holding one of those heavy duty Magic Wand vibrators against my pelvic bone. Blood pooled in my lower body and my panties grew damp as we continued to stare at each other. Pressing my thighs together, I bit my lip to keep from moaning.

"Excuse me, are you going to keep staring at your boy toy or help me check out?"

The harsh words broke the spell between us, and I stepped back, gasping for breath.

"I need to get back to work. Leave."

"As you wish, my mate."

From his dazed expression I had the impression that Ed was as flummoxed by what just happened as I was.

"When do you finish with your employment?" he asked.

"The library closes at eight," I said, then almost bit my own tongue out for that little slip.

"I will see you then, beautiful mate."

Ed strode away, and I rushed over to check out the impatient patron. I recognized her as one of the human women who lived just outside of town.

"Sorry for the delay, Mrs. Danielson."

"I understand the appeal dear – he really is a fine specimen—but that boy is way too young for you." Mrs. Danielson's face was pinched with disapproval. "Robbing the cradle is unbecoming for a woman your age."

The words stung, even as I reminded myself that Mrs. Danielson was one of those old ladies who was bitter and hated everyone. I knew that even if Ed was serious about wanting to be with me, I'd have to deal with people's poor opinions of our age gap anywhere I went.

Not that it was fair, of course. I didn't know for sure how much younger Ed was, but I was guessing about fifteen years, possibly twenty. Then again, I knew plenty of guys my age and older who dated women even younger than Ed. There was definitely a double standard at work.

Double standard or not, Ed being interested in me made no sense. Unless maybe all the women on his planet were old hags and I looked good in comparison? But there were plenty of hot young shifter women in town who would love to have even a night with a guy who looked like that.

You could just sleep with him. A voice sounded in my mind, but I was pretty sure it was my pussy talking. It was still throbbing with arousal from touching Ed.

The idea of sleeping with a studly young alien certainly had appeal, but what if he got attached? What if I did? What if he was serious about this soulmate thing? I was going to be the laughingstock of Greysden if I hooked up with such a young guy. I had to get rid of him before I did something stupid.

Edfollopxen

I returned to the library promptly at eight p.m., having set my comms to be on Earth time. The days on Earth were shorter than they were back on Genervia, where each day was closer to the equivalent of thirty Earth hours. It was amazing the inhabitants of this planet got anything done with such short time increments.

Marian was walking towards the front door when I entered. Her eyes widened when she saw me, and she seemed a bit nervous.

"Hey, I was just closing up, but why don't you come in for a second."

She moved past me, flipping the lock on the door and turning the sign from "open" to "closed".

"Are you ready for us to be mated now?" I asked her.

I knew the answer was no before she opened her mouth.

"I can't decide if you are really committed to this joke, or if you are actually serious, but either way, let me be clear, you and me, Ed? It won't work. There's no scenario where we will be together."

Her words wounded me, given that I could sense that she felt the same strong pull towards me that I felt for her. I'd talked to the Bear Man about it this afternoon, and Charlie explained that human women liked to be wooed. I wasn't sure what 'wooed' was, but I was committed to doing it if it meant that it would speed up my mating with Marian.

She stalked past me to the large desk where I'd seen her helping the customers. I followed her.

"Why do you say this won't work?" I asked, curious to get to the bottom of her resistance. "We are soulmates, Marian. We were meant to be together. You must feel the pull."

She spun around to face me, her eyes sparking with annoyance. My *afgha* twitched inside my new Earth-style pants. My mate was magnificent.

"First of all, you are way too young for me. I'm forty-five years old."

She said this like it meant something important. It took a second for the meaning of her words to sink in.

"Ah, so you are saying that it is forty-five times that the Earth has traveled around your sun then? That is how you measure biological age here, yes?"

Her eyes narrowed. "Yes."

"We count time differently on my home planet, but I believe...," I stopped to think for a moment. "Yes, that's right, in Earth years I believe I am about fifty-six."

Her jaw dropped. "You are not fifty-six."

"Indeed I am. If you would like to give me a writing utensil, I will demonstrate my mathematical computation to prove it to you."

"You look like you are twenty-five, not fifty-six," she insisted.

"My people age more slowly than humans, and our life spans are longer," I explained. "You may know that your shapeshifter neighbors are slower to age than humans as well."

She gave me a skeptical look but then moved onto her next argument. I had the impression that she'd worked hard to come up with a list to present to me.

"You live in another galaxy. I don't do long-distance relationships."

"Ah, this is not a problem, I assure you mate. I have already notified my family that I am moving to Earth to be with my soulmate. They are very excited for me."

Her eyes widened as I continued, "My mother is eager to meet you. When we visit my family on Genervia she will throw us a banquet to celebrate our union. We have many friends and family who will attend."

"What are you going to do for work if you live here?" she asked. "There's this thing called money and you need to have some to support yourself. I'm not going to be your sugar mama you know."

It took me a second to puzzle out the meaning of her words. Earth idioms were fascinating.

"I see, you are worried that I will not be a good provider, correct?"

She nodded.

"Do not fear, mate, I have talked to Charlie the bear man about this, and he introduced me to a very friendly wolf named Stuart Grey. Stuart has offered me a job building things. He was very impressed by my strength, which exceeds that of his shifter employees."

"I am ready for your next objection."

"I, uh..."

Seeing that my mate had run out of arguments, I stalked forward. She took a step back, her body coming into contact with the counter behind her. I placed one hand on either side of her on the wooden surface, trapping her.

Her eyes widened and I could see the pulse in her throat beating rapidly. The air around us was scented with her arousal.

"What are you doing?" she whispered unsteadily.

I lowered my head until I could rub my nose against the side of hers. "I must have a taste of you."

She pulled her head back, eyes comically wide. "You don't mean that literally, do you?"

"Marian, right now I want nothing more than to rub my tongue over every inch of your delectable body and then mate with you until we are both completely sated."

She licked her lips, and my eyes tracked the motion. The ambient temperature of the air in our vicinity seemed to increase from the heat of our bodies.

"Are your species and mine even compatible? Sexually, I mean?"

I ran my tongue along the shell of her ear. She shivered.

"My people have found many soulmates on this planet, yes. It is why I started my search for a soulmate here," I explained. "There are some differences in our physiologies, but as I understand it, Earth women quite like it."

Before she could say anything else, I pressed my lips against hers. Only our lips were touching, but I could feel the impact of the touch throughout my body. Maybe Marian could too, because she sighed, then slid her tongue along the seam of my mouth. I opened, and to my surprise, she slipped her tongue into my mouth, sliding against my own.

So this is kissing, I thought.

I'd never kissed a female before, wanting to wait for my soulmate, but instinct took over, telling me what to do. As I kissed her back, our movements becoming increasingly rough, I pulled Marian closer until the soft pillows of her breasts pressed against my upper belly.

When we pulled apart, we were both breathing heavily. The pupils of Marian's eyes were so wide they almost swallowed the brown ring around them.

"Ed, what are you doing to me?" Marian whispered. "Everywhere you touch seems to vibrate through my body."

Ah yes, I'd forgotten that the vibration, something we called *praxorel*, was unique to our species. One friend who had found a mate on Earth had told me during a visit back to Genervia that only small felines could make this vibration on Earth.

"It drives the females wild," he'd confided in me. *"They use tiny machines to make those vibrations in their afghaxoya."*

Before she could say anything more, I wrapped my hands around Marian's waist and lifted her to sit on top of the counter. She widened her legs and I moved in between them. Marian leaned back on her hands, watching me carefully.

"What are you doing?" she asked breathlessly.

"I wish to taste your *afghaxoya*," I told her as I slid up her long skirt, revealing soft skin and shapely thighs.

She was wearing a strange covering over her *afghaxoya*, very different from Genervia where we didn't normally wear undergarments.

"Afgha-what?" she asked.

I ripped her undergarment off, and she gasped. "Oh. You want to go down on me? Wow, okay."

Tossing the scrap of fabric to the side, I slid her butt towards the end of the counter and pulled her legs onto my shoulders. I looked down at her *afghaxoya,* my mouth watering. I'd seen pictures of this body part on my own species, but Marian's was smoother, with only a patch of hair near her apex, and a pinkish color similar to the skin of her lips.

Guided purely by instinct, I leaned down and licked her from the bottom of her slit to the top. Marian made a little noise that I took as pleasure, and I repeated the motion several times.

"Oh my God, is your tongue vibrating in my pussy?" she gasped. "How are you doing that?"

"It is a skill of my people," I answered. "We call it the *praxorel.* It is something that happens when we are aroused."

My *afgha* was swollen and hard, pressing against the thin fabric of my pants. I felt an overwhelming urge to release it and rut into her like an animal, but my desire to pleasure my mate held my baser urges at bay.

My mate's *afghaxoya* was dripping with a delicious cream that I could not get enough of. The taste of her was intoxicating.

I realized that when I licked around the little lump at the very top of her *afghaxoya* Marian's legs tightened around me and her breathing quickened, so I focused my attention on that area.

My mate's tiny fingers came to my head, pulling sharply on my hair while she thrashed beneath me making the cutest little moaning noises.

"There," she ordered. "Right there. Yes, just like that, but harder."

Glad that my mate was able to instruct me in how to best please her, I deepened the pressure, circling the nub with my tongue until Marian suddenly stiffened.

"Ed!" Her nickname for me sounded like it was ripped from her very lungs. "Oh my God! Ed!"

Suddenly her back arched on the counter and she began to shake and shudder beneath me. I'd spent enough time pleasuring myself to recognize the signs of orgasm. I gripped her round hips to hold her in place and continued to lick her *afghaxoya*. A rush of new moisture flooded her center, and I lapped it up like the sweetest cream.

When she finally stopped shaking, I lifted my head to gaze upon my soulmate. Marian lay there breathing heavily, her eyes fixed on the ceiling. Eventually she pushed herself up to her elbows and met my eyes. She looked the way my mother looked when she drank too much *qwixel* wine, soft and happy.

"Holy shit, you're really good at that."

I felt a sense of pride at pleasing my mate so thoroughly.

"I am glad I pleased you. This was my first time doing this act, but I commit to you that I will get even better with practice."

She sat up so quickly she almost fell off the desk.

"Wait, that was your first time going down on a woman?" she asked incredulously. "How is that possible? No beginner is that good at that."

"My people do not engage in sexual activities until we meet our soulmates. There is no sense in doing these things with someone we are not meant to be together with for our lifetimes."

"Wait, you're not saying you're actually a virgin, are you?"

My mind converted the strange word to my own language as I tried to grasp her meaning.

"If you are asking if I have had sexual relations with another female, the answer is no. I have been waiting to find you, Marian, to partake of these particular pleasures."

"A fifty-six year old alien virgin," she mused, dropping down to her back again and staring up at the ceiling. "Damn. I can't wait to see what you can do after some practice."

Marian

I had never been so discombobulated in my entire life. I'd had guys go down on me many times over the years, and some were better than others, but Ed was on a whole different level. That long, rough tongue with the vibrations – it was like the best toy ever. Laying on the counter, naked from the waist down, I couldn't summon the energy to move.

And this guy was a virgin? That didn't seem possible.

After a few minutes, Ed leaned over me, looking concerned. "Have I damaged you, my mate?"

I pushed up to a seated position, making a mental note to sanitize the surface before I left for the night.

"No, I'm just...recovering."

I looked around, remembering that we were at the library. Holy cow, I'd let an alien go down on me at work. What was wrong with me? Greysden was pretty liberal about things like sex and nakedness, given that it was a shifter town, but surely the board would frown on this behavior from their head librarian? Thank God there were no security cameras in here.

What was wrong with me? A sexy blue man says I'm his mate and next think I know I'm acting like a needy slut. My face flamed with shame at my behavior.

"Look, thanks for the orgasm and all, but I shouldn't be doing things like this at work."

I dropped to my feet, pulling my skirt down, then grabbed my ripped panties from the floor, shoving them inside the cup of my bra so I could dispose of them at home.

I'd never had a man rip my underwear off my body like that. My entire body felt flushed at the memory. I wanted more. I needed more.

I knew this was probably a really bad idea, especially with this guy thinking I was his mate and him being a virgin and all, but I hadn't had sex in two years. If the full monty was as good as this preview had been, my new alien friend promised to be a wild ride. One I couldn't resist.

"Um. Do you want to come back to my place for a while?" I asked. "We could have dinner and finish what we started here."

I'd never seen anyone look so happy to spend time with me before.

"Yes, I would be very pleased to visit your abode."

I smirked at Ed's phrasing. He spoke like he'd learned English from a textbook from the 1800s.

"Hey, how do you know English?" I asked.

He tapped his right ear. "We all have universal translators implanted. Our people do a lot of business with other worlds, and this makes it easier."

"But how do you speak English to me?" I pressed. "I don't have a translator."

"I have studied many Earth languages on my way here from Genervia. I am also fluent in Russian, Cantonese, Spanish, and German."

"How long was the trip?" I asked in surprise.

"About six months in Earth time."

"You learned five languages in six months?" I asked incredulously.

He shrugged. "My people have a gift for language."

"Wow, okay."

After cleaning the counter with copious amounts of sanitizer, I locked up the library and headed towards my house on foot.

"It's about a ten minute walk," I told Ed.

Greysden was incredibly safe, the kind of place where people didn't even lock their doors, so I thought nothing of walking the half mile home from work each night. Ed fell into step beside me, his shoulder brushing mine as we walked.

The streets were quiet, with most people either spending time at home or going for runs in the nearby forest.

"This is me," I said as Ed and I reached the small two-bedroom bungalow I had purchased with my relocation allowance. It was a bit dated, but it had a huge backyard, and the price was right.

I unlocked the door, then stopped and turned to face Ed. "Just so we don't have any misunderstandings here, I'm offering you one night, that's it. Then you're going to have to hit the road, because I can't commit to anything more."

Besides, you'll find someone younger and hotter the longer you stay in town, I added silently.

"I will do whatever you wish, mate, even apply blunt force to the road, although I'm not sure what that might accomplish."

I opened my mouth to explain, then decided against it. He'd figure out English slang soon enough. I pushed open the door, stepping aside so Ed could follow me inside.

"Felix, I'm home!"

Behind me I felt Ed stiffen. "You already have a male?"

Just then my orange tabby came slinking over. I picked him up, kissing his furry forehead. He purred in my arms, the motion reminding me of how Ed vibrated earlier.

"Hey baby, mommy's home," I greeted my cat. "Ed, this is Felix. He's the only male in my life right now."

"Is this creature a feline?" he asked curiously.

"Yes."

Ed reached out his hand, then snatched it back as Felix hissed at him.

"He gets a little jealous," I explained. "He's very attached to me."

Setting Felix down on the floor, I turned back to Ed. "Are you hungry? Do your people eat?"

He looked offended. "Of course we eat. We are not cyborgs."

Felix meowed once, then wandered off, his interest in us already gone.

"Well, I was going to just heat up some leftover beef stew that I made yesterday. Does that sound okay?"

"I do not know this beef stew, but I am sure that I will like anything that you have made."

Somehow Ed made even the simplest statement sound like a declaration of love. I pushed that thought out of my head and got to work heating up dinner.

It was a surreal experience having a large blue alien sitting in my kitchen eating leftover beef stew with bread. He watched me carefully, mimicking my use of the spoon.

"This is a helpful thing," he said as he scooped up some broth.

"You don't use spoons on Genervia?" I asked.

"We would drink this like your latte," he explained.

"You can do that if you prefer," I said. "I'm not fancy."

"This is quite delicious, Marian," he told me. "It is similar to a dish we make at home using the meat from a wild *brxlyo*."

We ate in silence for a few minutes before I asked the question that had been bothering me.

"Do you really think we are soulmates?" I asked. "I know the shifters believe that kind of thing but if you are from a more advanced society, how can you possibly believe in fate?"

Ed put down his spoon, his intense eyes studying me carefully.

"My people are more technologically advanced than your Earth people, this is true. Part of our learning is that there are forces in the universe that even the most sentient beings cannot understand. One of those things is the biological and emotional connection that occurs only with a fated mate."

His gaze speared mine.

"Throughout our history, only the luckiest Genervians have been granted soulmates. Now that I have found you, I too am one of the luckiest Genervians. I promise to you that I will spend the rest of my life making you happy."

I wanted to believe him, I really did. His handsome face looked sincere and guileless. But if there was one thing I'd learned after forty-five years on this Earth, it was that something that sounded too good to be true was always going to disappoint me.

"I don't buy it," I said.

His brow crinkled. "I did not ask you to purchase anything."

"No, I mean I don't believe in soulmates. I don't believe in fate. And I really don't believe in happily ever afters."

He looked stricken for only an instant, then his face hardened with a stubborn resolve.

"In that case, I will endeavor to change your mind."

Edfollopxen

I looked into my soulmate's eyes, seeing the fear that lurked beneath her stern expression. I wondered why my mate was so disbelieving. It had to be the fact that she was a full human. I had met many creatures in this small town over the last three days, and most of them seemed to embrace the mystical world. And believing in fate and soulmates was part of that. But not my Marian.

She might not believe in fate and soulmates, but that was okay. I believed enough for both of us. Never in the history of Genervian people had fate made a mistake, and I was quite sure it wasn't going to start now.

We finished up the excellent dish that Marian called "stew" and loaded the dishes and utensils into the dish cleanser. It was very different from the dish cleansers we had on Genervia which cleaned with a kind of ionic mist, but I would guess hot water worked as well.

"I want to try kissing again," I told my mate as we finished our task. I felt gratified when I scented her instant arousal. "I liked it very much."

Moving closer, I placed one hand on her hip, one hand in the soft strands of her hair. I pressed my lips firmly against hers, then experimentally ran the tip of my tongue against the seam of her lips. She opened her mouth immediately, and I slid my tongue into her mouth and rubbed it against hers, much as she'd done for me earlier. It was quite nice.

Her fingers tightened at my waist and my *afgha* grew hard in my trousers. I pressed it against her upper belly, seeking relief. I could have kissed her all night, but Marian pulled away, breathing heavily.

"Let's take this into the bedroom," she whispered.

Her beige cheeks were tinged pink now, and I wondered if that was what happened to human women when they got excited.

She took my hand and led me to her bedchamber. I looked around curiously. The bedchambers on Genervia were generally very plain, holding only a bed, a wardrobe, and a small table with a lamp.

Marian's room was filled with color, from the fabric covering the large bed to the window coverings and the seating area she had set up in one corner. The bed was large for just one small human, but most confusing was the number of pillows atop her bed. There had to be at least eight pillows of different sizes.

"Does someone share this bed with you?" I asked, feeling the same pull of jealousy that I'd felt earlier when she'd called out Felix's name.

She gave me a strange look. "I wouldn't be sleeping with you if I wasn't single."

I didn't want to offend her, so I did not ask any more questions about the pillows, most of which she tossed on the floor next to the bed.

Marian removed her clothes, starting with her shirt and skirt, then moving to the bands of fabric that covered her breasts. I caught my breath as she revealed her soft and curvy body.

I stepped closer, mesmerized by her large and pendulous breasts, tipped with a dark pink. I ran one finger across the tip and she shuddered. Cupping my hands over her breasts, I gave them each an experimental squeeze. They were very pale, almost translucent, and much softer than I had expected. Touching them made my *afgha* twitch.

"How about you ditch those clothes?" she asked breathlessly.

Seeing my confusion, she amended, "Take off your clothes. I don't like being the only person naked."

That I understood. I removed my shirt, baring my chest, and my mate stared at me, looking pleased. I confess that I flexed my chest muscles, showing off for her. Then I removed my pants, freeing my *afgha*. Her eyes widened.

"Wow, you're freaking huge."

I looked down at my erect member. "I assure you, I am an average size for a Genervian man."

"Well, I bet there are a lot of happy Genervian women then."

"Our mates are satisfied, yes."

She stepped forward, wrapping her tiny hand around me as far as it would go. My *afgha* twitched in her hand.

"Holy shit, it's bumpy," she said in a surprised tone.

"Our *afgha* grows bumps when we are aroused. It heightens pleasure."

"Good Lord."

She was staring at my *afgha*, her eyes wide. I could not interpret her expression.

"Does my appearance displease you?" I asked.

"No, not at all. That's the best cock I've ever seen."

"You believe my *afgha* looks like a bird?" I asked, trying to recall what I'd learned about cocks.

She giggled and the sound was like music to my ears.

"Cock is English slang for penis. We also use dick."

Her fingers were sliding up and down my *afgha*, heightening my excitement. It felt completely different from when I did it for myself. Her touch was softer and gentler than my own, but quite pleasurable.

"Ah. So my *cock* pleases you?"

"Hell yeah," she said enthusiastically. "Let's take it for a ride and see if it's as good as it looks."

She backed up towards the bed, then climbed on top, settling on her back with her legs parted. I could see the moisture glistening on the folds of her pink *afghaxoya*. I stalked towards her, stopping at the foot of the bed.

"What do you call this?" I asked, pointing at her center.

"Pussy. Vagina, vag, vajayjay, muff, beaver, lady bits," she recited. "Oh, and cunt, but don't use that word, women hate it."

"Your language has many words for the same thing," I noted as I lowered myself to the bed.

"Yeah, we like our slang."

I lay down on top of Marian, rubbing my cock against the outside of her *afghaxoya* as I kissed her. I loved the feeling of our skin sliding against each other, it was incredibly erotic. Our kisses turned rougher, and my mate dug her fingers into my hair and pulled it hard enough to sting. I found I quite liked this sensation.

My entire body was vibrating with need, literally, thanks to the *praxorel,* and I knew that Marian felt the vibrations everywhere our bodies touched.

"You're like one of those vibrating beds they used to have in cheap hotels when I was younger," she laughed.

Later I would ask for an explanation of her strange simile, but at the moment I was feeling a tingling traveling down my spine and to my balls, telling me that my orgasm was close. I knew from research that it was rude for me to find my release before my mate did, so I resolved to help her achieve completion as quickly as possible.

I grabbed my cock and slid it through her folds until I found her opening, then pushed the tip inside her. She was surprisingly tight and also quite warm.

Marian took a deep, shuddering breath, and her channel opened more for me, allowing me to slide in more deeply. I moved slowly, careful not to hurt here, and when I was fully seated inside her heat, we both exhaled.

"My God," she panted, "between your size and those bumps on your cock, it feels like you're splitting me in two."

"Is that possible?" I asked in alarm, holding myself completely still. "You appear very delicate, but I understood that our physiology is quite compatible."

"It's just a turn of phrase. A women's vagina can expand enough to birth a child, and your cock isn't quite *that* big."

Unsure what to do next and not wanting to hurt my tiny mate, I balanced myself over her on my forearms waiting for instructions.

"You can move now," she told me, giving my ass a little slap with her hand.

Instinct took over, and I began thrusting my hips, sliding in and out of her heat. Marian wrapped her legs around my waist, tilting her pelvis, and I picked up speed. Her heavy breasts were bouncing beneath me, and she was making little sighing noises. The need to come inside her was strong.

Marian slid her hand between us, fingers going to her apex.

"Do you need to be touched there to reach completion?" I asked, determined to learn everything I could about bringing her pleasure.

"I'm so close, I just need a little...bit...more."

I pushed her fingers away, using my own to press against the nub that I had teased with my tongue earlier tonight. Meanwhile I continued pounding into her hard enough that we were sliding upwards on her large bed. Marian stretched her arms up, bracing her palms against the wall to prevent her from slamming her head.

When I pinched her nub between my fingers Marian's inner muscles fluttered, then tightened around my *afgha*. Her back arched, pressing her breasts against me, and a flood of moisture surrounded me.

"Ed!"

My mate was beautiful when she came. Her eyes were closed, her skin was flushed, and she appeared to be experiencing ecstasy.

When my mate stopped shuddering with her orgasm, I released her nub and succumbed to my primal instincts. I was moving fast now, pounding into her, desperate to mark her as mine.

And then it happened – for the first time in my life, I released my seed into something besides my own hand.

"Marian. My soulmate!"

I nearly wept from the feeling of joy that filled my body. I punched my hips back and forth rapidly, pressing in deep and filling her with my seed until I was totally empty. Only then did my muscles relax.

I rolled to my side, mindful of crushing my mate with my heavier weight, and pulled Marian into my arms, keeping my *afgha* inside her. It continued to twitch and vibrate, triggering answering spasms deep inside my mate.

"That was even better than I ever imagined," I told her.

"You did okay for a virgin," Marian said, but I already knew her well enough to know that the tone she used meant she was teasing me.

"The next time will be even better," I promised.

The mate bond would be fully activated by then, heightening our pleasure, but before I could explain that Marian yawned tiredly. When my mate fell asleep with her head on my chest, I felt like the luckiest male in the universe.

Marian

I woke up with a start several hours later. I was laying on top of Ed like I was a freaking blanket, his huge arms wrapped around me. I ran my hand down his chest to his abs, feeling the texture of his skin, so different from a human. It almost reminded me of the skin on the bottom of my cat's paws, soft but also the tiniest bit rough.

I probably should tell Ed to leave—I should have kicked him out after our first round—but damned if I didn't want to have an encore with my hunky alien. I knew that this couldn't last beyond tonight, and I was determined to enjoy it as much as I could while it lasted.

"You are restless, little mate. Tell me why."

Ed's voice was a little scratchy, as if he too had just woken up.

"I want you again," I told him.

In two seconds flat I was laying on my stomach. Ed hopped off the bed and pulled on my feet, sliding me towards the edge of the mattress.

"Quit manhandling me," I laughed, even though I secretly liked it.

"You will get on your hands and knees please," he said politely. "I feel compelled to take you from behind."

"Okay but make sure you get the right hole," I cautioned, remembering that until a few hours ago he'd been a virgin. "You are way too big to go into the back door without a lot of lube and preparation."

"I do not understand."

I looked over my shoulder at him so I could make sure he got my meaning. "You should fuck my pussy, not my asshole please."

He froze behind me, mouth opening in shock.

"Humans copulate in the *yaskcovar*?" I asked in shock. "You can get pregnant that way?"

"No, it's not for making babies, it's just something that some people think feels good. Not everyone likes it though."

"Hmm, I have not heard of this. I am not sure that I understand the appeal of such actions."

"Well, I can take it or leave it myself, but if you've never heard of anal, I have a feeling you're going to be super excited about blow jobs."

"Blow jobs?" he asked curiously.

"I'll explain later," I said. "Right now I need to feel you inside me."

'Need' was an understatement. I was practically vibrating with need for this man. I'd never been such a horny mess in my life.

Ed stepped closer, and I could feel his hardened cock slide along my pussy lips. He was doing that vibrating thing again, making it feel like he was using a toy instead of his cock.

"You look very beautiful in this submissive position," he told me, just before he shoved his cock into my channel in one long push. I made a squealing noise at the intrusion.

Ed grabbed my ass cheeks and began pounding into me. It was a good thing I liked my sex a little rough, because this dude was all enthusiasm and no finesse right now. I hadn't been with a virgin since I was a freshman in college. I'd forgotten that they needed a little help now and then.

"Ed, wait!" I called over my shoulder. "I'll push back when you push forward, so we can get into the same rhythm. Start a little slower and try not to knock me over. It'll help if you hold my hips instead of my butt."

He was a quick study, and soon we were completely in sync. My breasts swayed beneath me as I pushed back to meet his steady thrusts. It was rare for me to come without any direct clitoral stimulation, but Ed's cock was brushing against my G-spot, and that was enough to send me right over the edge, screaming his name as I came.

I was still quivering with aftershocks when Ed leaned over my back, bracing his hands outside my shoulders, and came inside me with a shout. I felt a pinch of pain and realized that he'd gripped a bit of my shoulder with his teeth, biting down hard enough to break the skin.

The bite triggered another orgasm, this one harder than the last. Every nerve ending in my entire body seemed to light up at once and

I shrieked from the sensation. I was not normally a shrieker, but surrounded by Ed, feeling the twin sensations of pain and pleasure, I came harder than I'd ever come in my life.

When it was over, I collapsed onto the bed, bringing Ed with me. His bulk pressed me into the mattress.

"Can't. Breathe." I mumbled, and he rolled to the side.

I heaved in a huge breath as I felt his lips teasing the bite mark on the top of my shoulder.

"I can't believe you bit me," I groused. "What are you, a damned wolf?"

"I am Genervian," he replied, his voice puzzled. "You know this."

I rolled over to sit up, feeling along the wound at the base of my neck. It was larger and deeper than I realized. It was probably going to scar.

"You bit me like a shifter. What the hell?"

"Much like the shape shifters of your world, my people mark each other to let others know that they are mated," he explained. "After the bond has fully strengthened, I will be able to locate you at all times, no matter how far we are separated. We will also be better able to sense each other's emotions now that we are officially mated. It will help us grow closer emotionally."

Pure panic filled me.

"Wait a damn minute, are you saying that you mated me against my will and implanted me with some kind of Genervian GPS in my shoulder?"

"What's a gee-pee-ess?" he asked.

"It's a tracking system."

"Ah yes, it works like that, yes," he confirmed.

"I did not give you permission to mate me, or to put a tracker in me. Undo it. Now."

He looked confused.

"Why are you angry with me, mate?" he asked. "I thought you understood what the Genervian mating entails."

"How?" I yelled, getting off the bed and grabbing some lounge pants and a sweatshirt from the drawer and pulling them on. "I never even freaking heard of Genervia until yesterday."

"But you invited me into your bed chamber and encouraged me to mate with you."

"No," I yelled, "I invited you to fuck me."

"This is the same thing," he said in a calm voice that irritated me even more.

"No it's not!" I yelled. At this point my voice was so high-pitched I was expecting the neighbor's dog to start howling at me.

"You're going to need to get out of here before I do something we both regret."

"But, mate…"

I pointed at the door. "Get. Out. Now!"

I felt a wave of sadness that I realized was coming from Ed. Damn it, I had enough trouble managing my own emotions without managing his too. He got up off the bed and pulled his own clothes on, looking at me like I was the person who'd run over his puppy. Or whatever animals they kept as household pets on freaking Genervia.

I couldn't decide if I wanted to punch something or burst into tears.

"I will leave you for now," he finally said, and I realized he was probably feeling my emotions as well. "While we are apart, I will endeavor to understand why I made you so angry and I will make things better so we can live together forever."

I pointed at the door. "Go!"

As he obeyed my order and left me alone, I couldn't decide which of us was sadder.

Edfollopxen

I lay on the bunk of my ship, mentally reviewing everything that had happened with Marian since I'd arrived at the library last night. I remembered clearly saying that I wanted to mate with her, although it appeared that she did not fully comprehend what that entailed.

Although maybe the part where she said she only wanted one night was a hint. Biting her had been instinctual, but then again, I would have thought that after our life-changing copulation, she was no longer wanting only one night.

Our mate bond was still forming but even across town I could feel a connection to her. I was sure she could as well. I knew that even though the bond was more noticeable with Genervians, the humans could still feel it, but not quite as strong.

I was hurt and confused by Marian's rejection, and unsure what to do about it. Glancing at my comms, I realized I should get some rest. I was starting my new job in the morning, and I wanted to impress my shifter boss. Continued employment would ensure that when I worked things out with Marian, I would be able to provide for her properly like a good mate.

By the end of my first day of work I had several new friends. My 'crew' as they were called, was working together to build a house. There were only males on the crew, most of them wolves or bears.

"The vamps and the fae all think they're too good for manual labor," my foreman told me.

Frank was an older bear shifter who informed me that he was "counting down the days until retirement". I wasn't sure what that meant but I was planning to look it up later.

"Hey Big Blue," Frank called to me at the end of the day.

I looked behind me, then realized he was talking to me.

"Yes boss?" I addressed him as I'd heard the others on my crew do.

"You did a great job today. Why don't you come to Murphy's with the crew for a beer?"

"You are inviting me to attend your social gathering?" I clarified.

Frank chuckled like I'd said something entertaining. "Yeah, come on, I'll buy you a beer to celebrate your first day of work."

Murphy's Bar was a large bar in downtown Greysden. It had scarred hardwood floors, a long bar, and a mix of tables and booths to sit at. I liked it immediately. When I entered the bar with the crew, I got a few curious looks but overall the vibe here was friendly.

I immediately noticed the woman who had been with my mate the day I found her. She was sitting at a table with three other women. Based on their appearance, I assumed that they were related.

"Excuse me," I said to Frank. "I must say hello to my mate's friend."

"You have a mate?" Frank asked in surprise. "You've been here a few days. You move fast, my man."

"As the humans would say, it's a long story."

I headed to the table, my approach immediately catching the woman's attention.

"Hello again, female. You are a friend of my mate, Marian. I apologize that I was so distracted when I found her that I did not get your name."

Before my mate's friend could respond, the other women burst out laughing. I looked at them in confusion, wondering what I'd said that was amusing.

"Oh Pepper, it happened again?" one female asked. "You were with someone who found their mate?"

Pepper rolled her eyes. "You know me, I'm a mate magnet. For everyone except myself of course."

She gave me a friendly smile.

"Hi, I'm Pepper Rosewater. These are my sisters Meri and Cami, and my cousin Jane."

"My name is Edfollopxen, but my friends call me Ed," I greeted them.

"How are things going with Marian?" Pepper asked.

"I am afraid she is currently angry with me." I couldn't keep the sorrow out of my voice. "She has told me to stay away from her and is rejecting our mate status."

The young woman who had teased Pepper about being with Marian when we met lifted her hand towards me, an intense expression on her pretty face.

"May I?"

I nodded, unsure what I was agreeing to. The young woman wrapped her hand around my wrist and closed her eyes, taking a deep breath.

"Are you getting anything, Meri?" Pepper asked.

Meri opened her eyes and released me. "Your mother will call you tonight to tell you news about your sister."

I looked at her in confusion. "What news? And how do you know this?"

"She's a psychic," Pepper explained. "Although I think she was trying to get a better read on your situation with Marian, not give you a heads up about your mother calling."

Meri shrugged. "I can't control the psychic flashes, just share them when they come."

Out of the corner of my eye I saw Frank waving at me.

"I must return to my crew now."

"Your crew?" Pepper turned around to see what I was looking at. "Oh, are you working at Grey Construction?"

"Yes, Marian will not be a sugar mama, so I need to have employment."

The women all burst out laughing.

"Have fun with your buddies, Ed," Pepper said. "I'm sure we'll see you around."

I joined my coworkers at a large table in the back of the bar where they introduced me to a human drink called 'beer'. It had a distinctive taste that was similar to a fermented beverage we had back on Genervia, and I quite liked it. It went well with the large baskets of 'french fries' that someone had ordered for the group.

I was drinking my second beer when I felt a humming beneath my skin. My mate was nearby. My head whipped around just as the heavy door opened and Marian walked into the bar.

"There she is," I told Frank, nodding toward the door. "There's my beautiful human mate."

Marian

I stepped into Murphy's Bar, looking around for Pepper and her sisters. I was finishing up my shift at the library when I received Pepper's text insisting that I come to Murphy's and meet them for a drink.

It had been a long hard day that was even more difficult due to my having a sleepless night. After I'd kicked out Ed I'd tossed and turned, unable to sleep as I obsessed about my suddenly not-exactly-single status. A night out with the girls would do me good.

Pepper waved from a table in the center of the room, and I headed in her direction. Suddenly I felt a...sensation. I couldn't quite explain it, but I knew that Ed was nearby. Sure enough, when I glanced towards the back of the bar, Ed was there with a bunch of local guys.

I wasn't sure how he knew them, and I wasn't going to ask.

To my surprise, Ed merely gave me a smile and a nod. That was weird, I thought for sure he'd come over here and bug me. Instead, he was over there playing it cool with his friends. I wasn't sure why that bothered me, but it did.

"Hey Marian," Pepper greeted me. "Glad you could make it."

I joined the Rosewater women at the table. Pepper slid an empty glass towards me, and Meri poured me some of the margarita that was in a pitcher in the middle of the table. My friends were watching me intently, which immediately made me suspicious of this sudden invitation.

"Did you know that Ed was here when you invited me?"

"What's the big deal? You rejected him, right?"

I pinned Pepper with a suspicious look. "How do you know that?"

"He told us."

I took a huge sip of my margarita. When I looked up, everyone at the table was staring at me.

"Might as well spill it," Pepper's cousin Jane said. "Pepper will get it out of you eventually. Save yourself the trouble."

I glanced over to where Jane's mate was sitting at the table with Ed. "How does Gabe know my, um, how does he know Ed?"

"They're working on the same crew at Grey Construction," she replied. "They brought Ed in to celebrate his first day of work. Now quit stalling and tell us what happened with your big blue mate."

I gave them a high level overview of Ed's visit to the library yesterday – skipping over the part where he ate me out on the circulation desk – and shared how I'd invited him home for dinner.

"Then we...," I looked around to make sure no one could hear us, "started fooling around and he marked me! Apparently he can track me now or something."

I glanced over at Ed's table and saw him looking at me with concern, making me wonder if he was sensing my agitation. I took a deep breath as he returned his attention to his new friends.

"Wait, he marked you without permission?" Cami asked. "That's not cool."

"Well, we might have had a miscommunication," I admitted reluctantly. "He said he wanted to mate me, but he has this old fashioned way of talking, you know? So when he said that I thought he meant have sex, not tie us together forever."

"Are you going to see him again?" Jane asked. "If it works anything like how it does for the shifters, you're going to have a hard time staying away from each other."

"I don't know. Please, can we talk about something else? Anything else?"

I spent another ninety minutes hanging out with the Rosewaters before I settled my share of the tab and headed home. Ed didn't approach me while I was there, but I was aware of him the entire time, and I knew that he was keeping his attention on me as well.

He followed me home, walking maybe a block behind me, like a big blue bodyguard, and when I looked out the window after I got into the house, I saw him standing by my driveway. After a few minutes he walked slowly away, his entire posture dejected.

Exhaustion overtook me and I practically passed out on my bed, not even bothering to get undressed.

***

I'm walking down Main Street in Greysden. Half a block ahead of me I see a little boy, he's maybe three, suddenly he bursts out of his clothes and turns into a wolf. I can't help but laugh as he runs towards me at full speed. These little shifters sometimes struggle to contain their dual natures, which is why Greysden is such a great place for them to live. No one bats an eye here when someone turns furry.

Suddenly he veers to the right, darting between two parked cars, right into oncoming traffic. The driver doesn't see him. There's a sickening crunch....

***

I woke up in a cold sweat, my breath coming in short anxious bursts. *It was just a nightmare,* I told myself, looking around my bedroom to ground myself. But it felt so real, like it was a memory and not a dream. Wide awake, I decided to get up. I'd fallen asleep fully dressed, so I pulled on a pair of shorts and a tank top before going into the kitchen to make myself a cup of chamomile tea. Hopefully the tea would help me get sleepy again.

I was standing by the counter waiting for the kettle to boil when a rap on my back door made me jump.

"What the hell?"

Ed was standing on the other side of the glass, an intense expression on his face.

"What are you doing here?" I asked, pulling the door open just enough to talk to him.

"What is wrong, mate? You were upset."

I rolled my eyes as I realized that he must have felt the intense emotions that had accompanied the nightmare. Damned mate bond.

"I'm fine. I just had a nightmare."

He looked at me questioningly.

"A bad dream," I explained.

"I am glad you are not in danger as I thought," he said. "I will leave now."

I sighed. It was sweet of him to come over, and after such an intense dream, I wouldn't mind some company for a little while.

"Do you want to come in for a cup of tea?"

His face lit up. "Yes."

I made us each a cup of tea then brought them to the table. Ed watched me carefully as if he'd never steeped a teabag before. I supposed he hadn't. When I took a sip of my hot drink, he did the same, then grimaced.

"You don't like it?" I asked, rolling in my lips to keep from laughing.

"You have made it, so I like it," he said in a serious voice.

I shook my head. "Some faceless corporation made this, not me," I said. "Do you want water or a beer instead?"

Not that I'd been watching him at Murphy's Bar or anything, but it was possible that I'd noticed how much he'd seemed to enjoy beer. I knew I was right when his eyes lit up.

"Yes, beer is quite delicious!"

"Tell me how this mate bond works," I asked as I uncapped a bottle of beer and handed it to him. "How did you know I was having a nightmare?"

"I was sleeping, and I could feel your heart rate increase. I could sense that you were feeling scared, panicked maybe, and that your breath was not coming as easily. I came to you as quickly as I could."

I nodded. That sounded exactly like how I'd felt. As I took a sip of my tea, I felt myself grow sleepy again.

"Do you want to stay over?" I asked.

Edfollopxen

Before I could respond to my mate's invitation to slumber with her, she added, "Just to sleep. No funny business."

I must have looked confused because she explained, "No sex I mean. We'll just sleep. I need to work in the morning, and I imagine you do as well."

We finished our drinks, then took turns using the bathroom before heading into Marian's bedroom. I removed my garments and climbed into bed next to my mate. She was on her back, as far over on the side of the bed as she could be, but when I settled on my side, she scooted a bit closer. I felt her hand shift to the middle of the bed, her finger grazing my hip, then she stiffened.

"Where are your clothes?" she asked.

"We do not wear clothes to sleep like humans do," I replied.

She mumbled something under her breath, then pulled the bed covering up to her chin and closed her eyes. A few minutes later I heard her breath even out as she fell asleep. It was only then that I let myself relax.

When I woke up Marian was snuggled against me, her head on my shoulder, one arm tossed over my waist. One of her tiny little feet was tucked between my calves. It was surprisingly cold.

"Mmm."

My mate stirred to awareness, looking up at me with a sleepy expression. She looked adorable.

"I'm sorry, I totally got up into your space."

I wrapped my arm around her, pulling her close. "I am not sorry. I enjoy having you so close, mate."

Loud music erupted from her communications device on the bedside table. It was a song about 'getting physical', whatever that meant.

"Time to get up," she said, pushing away to silence her device. "Do you have time to stop at Bearly Beans for a coffee before we go to work?"

I nodded, pleased that my mate was interested in spending time with me. I got dressed while Marian cleaned up in the bathroom, emerging dressed in a tight skirt that hugged her curves and stopped at the knees.

"What do they call this?" I asked, pointing towards her bottom half.

"It's a pencil skirt," she said, smoothing down the fabric. "Why?"

"It is very sexy. I want to rip it off and mount you from behind."

Her face turned pink, and I smelled the sweet scent of her arousal in the air.

"Um. Well, we don't have time for that. I need caffeine before I go to work."

It was a clear, cool day outside and we walked side by side towards the downtown area where both Marian's library and the bear man's coffee shop was. We were about a block away when my mate gasped beside me.

I followed her gaze. A young boy was shifting into his wolf form and running up the sidewalk towards us, moving so quickly his little paws seemed to float above the sidewalk.

"I've got to stop him!"

Marian raced off, heading for the space between two cars. I saw why when the young pup veered off the sidewalk to run between them. She caught him by the hips, picking him up into her arms.

"You can't run into the street," she chided as a car came rumbling by, driving way too fast.

"Oh my God, Marian, thank you."

The pup's mother rushed over and gave her offspring a stern look as Marian set him back on his feet between them. The pup changed back into his human form as his mother pulled him close.

"You would have gotten hit by a car if Miss Marian hadn't stopped you. You tell her thank you."

"Thank you, Miss Marian."

After more effusive thanks, the mother and her pup departed. Marian sagged against the nearest car, looking disturbed.

"How did you know the tiny wolf was going to run into the street?" I asked curiously.

He'd been running straight up the sidewalk initially.

"It was in my dream," she said. "The one that woke us both up. I saw this. Like a premonition or something. That was so weird."

I pulled her close, wrapping my arms around her, relieved when she sagged against my chest with a sigh. We stood there for several minutes until she'd recovered from the excitement and was ready to go get her coffee.

"Can I ask you a question?" she asked as I walked her from the coffee shop to the library.

"Of course."

"When I saw you at Murphy's last night, I thought you'd come over to talk to me. Instead, you just watched me from across the room and then followed me home without talking to me. Why?"

I'd wondered if she knew I was walking behind her, ensuring that she returned to her residence unharmed.

"I talked with my new friends about my dilemma and sought their counsel."

"What dilemma?" she asked.

"The dilemma that I am being rejected by my fated mate," I explained. "My boss Frank said I must play hard with you and not approach you or act like a lovesick puppy."

She looked over at me, a puzzled expression on her face. "Play hard? You mean hard ball?" she asked.

I shook my head. That wasn't quite right.

"Oh, do you mean hard to get?" she asked.

"Yes, this is it. I am playing hard to get. This will make you wild with desire for me," I explained. "Frank also suggested that I pretend to be interested in another female to incite jealousy from you, but I was not comfortable with this suggestion. No other women are appealing to me, and I am not skilled in subterfuge."

We walked along in silence for a few minutes until I couldn't resist asking, "Is it working? Do you find me hard to get?"

Marian giggled, I wasn't sure why, but I quite liked the sound of it.

"It's working a little bit. Do you want to get together for dinner tonight after work?" she asked. "We could order pizza and watch a movie if you'd like."

I searched through my memory for the unfamiliar word. "I am unsure what pizza is."

"Well then, you are in for a treat. It's delicious. How about you come by my house at seven o'clock?"

"I will," I promised.

"Great, it's a date."

By the time I got to my job site, the news of Marian's rescue of the pup had spread all over town. I felt deep pride as my coworkers complimented my mate's fast reflexes.

"Your mate is a fast thinker," Frank said, giving me a slap on the shoulder. "Pretty and smart."

I felt a surge of jealousy at my boss's assessment of my mate's appearance but then I remembered that Frank had a mate of his own. His appreciation was purely platonic.

"How's it going with Marian anyway?" he asked. "I heard that you were with her when she rescued the pup."

"It is going better," I told him. "She has invited me to her abode to eat pizza this evening."

"That's promising all right. Now let's get some work done so you have time to clean up before your big date."

Marian

I couldn't stop thinking about the incident with the pup. All day I replayed that scene and wondered how my dream was related. I'd never dreamt of anything that came true before. Something about the whole situation was freaking me out, probably because every detail of the dream had been the same in real life.

By the time I was done with my shift at the library, I was ready to do something to put it out of my mind. Or do someone, as the case may be.

The more time I spent with Ed, the more I wanted him. I'd told us both that I didn't want to be his mate, but like an idiot, I kept inviting him to spend time with me. I had to admit, I'd loved sleeping in his arms last night. I loved waking up with him this morning. And I was starting to love the way he looked at me like I was the best thing in the universe.

Maybe this mate thing wouldn't be bad. Although we did get a few weird looks at Bearly Beans earlier. I wasn't sure if it was because I was obviously so much older than him, or if it was just that people were wondering why he was blue.

Then again, why did I care? I was a grown ass woman. If I wanted to have a relationship with Ed, I could do it. I just wasn't sure if I could trust my emotions. I wasn't sure if I could trust him. I hadn't ruled out the idea that this could all be some kind of elaborate prank, although that seemed less likely the more time I spent with Ed. He seemed incredibly sincere.

Ed knocked on my door promptly at seven o'clock. When I opened the door, he was standing there with a huge bouquet of flowers.

"For you, mate," he said, holding out the bouquet.

"It's beautiful," I said, sticking my nose in between the blooms and inhaling the sweet floral scents.

Ed beamed.

When I reached for the flowers, they scattered on the floor. I realized that the bottoms of the stems were all raggedy, as if they'd been torn from the ground. A few still had clumps of dirt attached to the bottoms.

"Um, Ed, where did you get these flowers?"

"I picked them for you on the way here," he said proudly. "Frank said that human women love flowers, and I remembered seeing many at the house on the corner."

I squatted down to pick up the flowers, then motioned him to follow me into the house.

"I appreciate the flowers so much," I started, making a mental note to call my neighbor to apologize for Ed ransacking her flower beds. "But just so you know, you can't just pick flowers from people's houses."

Ed frowned. "Why not? They are outside."

"Yes, but anything from the sidewalk to the house is private property." At his confused look I explained, "It means you can't be there or take anything without the permission of the owner."

"This is an Earth rule?"

I couldn't help but giggle at the confused look on his face.

"Yes."

"Okay, I will remember this. But where were the flowers that Frank said I should bring then?"

"There's a flower shop a few doors down from Bearly Beans," I explained. "He probably meant to go there. Let me go put these flowers in water."

After cutting the stems, I arranged the flowers in a large vase, setting it in the middle of the kitchen table.

"There you go, so beautiful."

"Yes."

When I looked up though, Ed was staring at me, not the flowers. I felt my cheeks warm. When I got home from work, I'd changed into yoga pants, a tank top, and a loose hoodie, then pulled my long hair into a messy bun. It was what I would wear for a night at home alone, and I'd resolved not to do anything special for Ed. If he liked me, he was going to have to like me just the way I was. Based on the looks he was sending me, he totally did.

When the pizza arrived, we settled on the living room couch to eat. I turned on a superhero movie but kept the volume low as we ate and talked about our day. I was impressed with how much Ed seemed to like his new job. It sounded like hard work, but I knew that Stewart Grey treated his staff well.

"This food is quite delicious," Ed said as he reached for his seventh piece of pizza.

It was a good thing I'd ordered an extra large.

We were sitting close together on the couch, and as the night wore on, we somehow seemed to be closer and closer even though I wasn't aware of either one of us moving. By the end of the movie, I was pressed up against Ed from shoulder to knee, and my body was vibrating with arousal. I was a needy mess. When I couldn't take it anymore, I turned off the television and gave Ed a long look.

"Do you want to stay over tonight?" I asked. My voice sounded sultry.

"You wish to sleep side by side again?" he clarified.

I shook my head, then nodded.

"I want to sleep together, yes, but first I want to ride you until both of us forget what day it is."

His brow wrinkled in confusion, so I decided to be clearer. "I want to fuck you."

"I like this idea," he said, a huge smile spreading across his blue tinted face. "My *afgha* has been hard all night."

My eyes dropped to his cock, confirming his statement. In one swift movement, he stood up, grabbed me around the waist, and tossed me over his shoulder.

"Ed!" I shrieked, "Put me down."

I have to admit that the girl in my thrilled at how easily he handled me. Ed hastened to the bedroom, his large strides eating up the space between rooms, and then he flipped me over to set me on my feet. Without a word, he grabbed my shoulders and pulled me close to him, his firm lips crashing down on mine.

Every cell in my body seemed to have a little celebration at once. I went from low level excited to burning up with passion in about five seconds.

Ed pulled my hair out of its bun, tunneling his fingers into my hair and tilting my head to get a better angle. Meanwhile, I slid my hands down his back and under his waistband, not stopping until I was squeezing the muscled globes of his bare ass.

"Mmm," I said as we pulled apart to catch our breath. "How about you get naked for me?"

I didn't have to ask him twice. Ed was naked before I'd even pulled my shirt over my head. He watched as I finished undressing, his gaze burning with desire. It did a lot for a woman's ego to be looked at that way, especially at my age.

"On your back," I said, pointing at the bed. "I want to be on top."

Ed looked slightly confused but followed my instructions without argument. My cat Felix, who was sleeping on one corner of the bed, meowed his displeasure then stalked off to find a new place to sleep.

"Lay your head on the pillows," I instructed Ed.

He scooted up until his big body was in the center of the bed. I followed him, crawling over his body until I was straddling his thighs. His cock was fully erect, bumpy and angry looking. My mouth watered, but I wanted him inside me. I reached up to tweak my nipples, gratified when I heard him groan in pleasure watching me.

"I want you," I told him.

"Please take me," he said politely.

I smothered a smile. "With pleasure."

Edfollopxen

I wasn't sure what this ritual was, but I definitely liked it. Marian was sitting on my thighs, her damp *afghaxoya* pressed against my naked skin. Her fingers were rubbing and teasing at her nipples, making them pop out into hard points.

Following my instincts, I sat up and took one in my mouth, suckling her. Marian gripped the back of my head, arching her back to encourage me to take more of her breast into my mouth. I gladly complied.

My *afgha* was as hard as the concrete I'd learned to pour at my job with Grey Construction. I wanted to flip Marian onto her hands and knees and rut into her from behind like we'd done the other night, but I was content to follow Marian's lead.

She pressed against my shoulders, encouraging me to lay back again, then lifted up on her knees and scooted upwards.

"I want you inside me," she said.

"I want this as well," I confirmed.

She smirked, although I wasn't sure what was amusing about my response. Then I forgot all about it as she grabbed my *afgha,* gave it several hard pumps, then lined it up with her opening.

"You ready?" she asked.

I nodded, unable to form English words right now due to all my blood pooling beneath my waist.

Marian lowered her body, taking me inside her body until I was fully seated inside her. We both groaned in pleasure. In this position I could see the contrast between her pale pink pussy and the blue of my own skin.

"I forgot how big you are," she said, almost as if she was talking to herself. "It's only been a few days but somehow I forgot. And the bumps..."

She braced her palms on my chest and began moving, sliding herself up and down my *afgha* at a steady pace. I moved to grab her hips, desperate to speed things up, but she smacked my hands away.

"Be a good boy and keep your hands behind your head," she ordered.

I quite liked it when Marian was bossy, so I complied with her instructions. She rewarded me by doing some kind of circling movement with her hips that almost made me come on the spot.

"Mate," I groaned.

She sped up her movements and soon I could feel the flutters deep inside her body that warned of her approaching orgasm.

"I'm close," she said, her voice a little high pitched. "Play with my tits."

When it was clear I didn't know this word, she clarified, "My nipples, play with my nipples. Squeeze them."

I caught the tips of her breasts between my fingers, rolling them and squeezing them as she requested until Marian screamed out my name and began shaking. This time I did grab her hips, holding her still while I bent my knees, braced my feet on the bed, and began thrusting my hips upwards.

Marian collapsed onto my chest, our bodies still connected, and I continued punching my hips upwards until I too reached completion. I whispered her name over and over again as I released my seed into her body, filling her with my essence.

When we were both sated, I rolled us to our sides, then found the blanket and pulled it up to cover us. I didn't need it, but I knew my mate felt cold without additional covering. I wanted her to be comfortable. She sighed softly, her eyes closed and her expression one of pure bliss as she relaxed into sleep.

I couldn't help but feel proud of my ability to please my mate.

I snoozed next to her for a while, Marian's back pressed against my front. Without any effort from me, my *afgha* was hardening again, pressing against her ass. I remained completely still, not wanting to disturb her for fear she'd kick me out again.

Eventually she came awake, her hips rolling back against me, rubbing her ass against my *afgha*. It was quite pleasant, but I wanted more, and so did Marian. She shifted a little closer.

"Put your top leg between mine," she instructed.

I complied with her request, separating her legs with mine.

"Now you can slide your cock inside me," she said. "Nice and slow."

I discovered that our new position did indeed make this possible. Slowly, as slowly as I could, I fed her my *afgha*. With her legs in this position, Marian seemed tighter. I grit my teeth to keep from moving as fast as my instincts were pushing me to do.

Marian pulled one of my arms under her head, then whispered, "Put your other arm around me."

"I am glad to do so," I told her, wrapping my arm around her curvy little body and cupping her breast in one hand.

She must have liked this because she made a happy little sound deep in her throat.

Marian began rolling her hips backwards and I soon caught onto the motion, rolling my own hips forward to meet her. She was still wet, sticky with our fluids from our earlier lovemaking, and there was a squelching sound as I pushed in and out of her.

"Oh my God, that feels so good," she whispered.

It didn't take long until my mate was spasming around me, and I soon followed her over the edge, taking my pleasure in her sweet body. We fell back asleep, our bodies still joined, and I slept more soundly than I had in my entire life.

When I woke up again, the sun was shining brightly and I was alone in bed. After using the toilet, I wandered into the kitchen to find Marian. She was drinking coffee and reading a book at the kitchen table, the flowers a riot of color in the center of the table. I made a mental note to thank Frank for his idea to bring my mate flowers.

"Good morning, sleepyhead," Marian teased.

"My entire body was sleeping," I said in confusion. "But it is fully awake now."

She laughed. "It's an expression. It means that you slept for a long time and woke up looking like you are still half asleep."

"Ah, I see. Yes, this term is accurate."

I moved behind her, wrapping my arms around her waist, and gave her a little squeeze. She leaned back with a sigh.

"Do you have to work today, mate?" I asked. "I am not working today."

"No, I don't work on Saturdays. I was planning to go the Greysden Farmer's Market and pick up some produce. Would you like to come along? We could stop at the diner on the way and have breakfast."

"I would like this very much."

Marian

The Diner was a Greysden institution. The place was run by Mr. and Mrs. Xenakis, a pair of mated badger shifters who traded gossip in between making the best breakfast in town.

Knowing that Ed was unfamiliar with most of our breakfast foods, I ordered two huge platters with an assortment of things for him to try. When the food arrived, I explained what each one was.

"What is this one? It smells delicious?"

"It's called bacon," I explained. "It's a cured meat made from pigs. It's heaven on Earth."

He frowned in confusion, then his face lightened as he ate an entire slice of bacon in one bite. "I understand your enthusiasm for this cured meat. It's quite tasty."

"Told ya," I teased, taking my own slice of bacon before he ate it all.

"Miss Marian!" Mr. Xenakis came to the table with open arms and a wide smile. He was a short man with hair that was mostly gray, and a stocky frame. "Is it true?"

I looked around, noticing that most of the people in the diner were staring at us now.

"Is what true?" I asked.

"This young blue man is your mate?"

"That's what he says."

"I am Ed," my dining partner reached out a hand towards Mr. Xenakis. "It is true that Marian is my mate."

Clearly one of his guy friends had taught him about handshakes.

"Ed, this is Mr. Xenakis. He and his wife own this diner."

"Our breakfast food is delicious," Ed told him politely.

Mr. Xenakis beamed. "I will tell my mate, she is cooking this morning."

"Thank you, young man," the woman in question called from the kitchen.

Shifter hearing was no joke. It was why you couldn't keep a secret in this town.

Ed and I finished our breakfast, mostly silent until we went to the cash register to pay our bill. Mr. Xenakis was there when we approached, frowning as he poked at the buttons.

"This damn thing," he muttered. "It made me change the password but now I can't remember what it was. I need to re-set it."

"It's capital C, lower case y-a-t, number 5, explanation point," I said automatically.

The shifter input the combination I suggested, then looked up at me in surprise. "How did you know that?"

"I dreamt it last night," I realized. "That's so weird. Why would I dream about a password I didn't know?"

I tried to brush it off, but over the next five days I had two more dreams that turned out to be premonitions. And despite my protestations about not wanting anything serious, I was dating my mate.

Ed and I got together every night, had mind blowing sex at least twice, then fell asleep in each other's arms. Sex had never been like this for me before, so intense, so satisfying. It was like we couldn't get enough of each other.

When we got up in the morning Ed would head back to his ship to get ready for his job at Grey Construction, then at night we'd meet up again and repeat our routine.

By unspoken agreement, we hadn't discussed what we were doing, but it was nice. Very nice. Despite my efforts to the contrary, I was getting attached to Ed, and he seemed to feel the same way. I was still worried that things would go south with him. Everything between us felt too easy. I kept waiting for the other shoe to drop. Like maybe one day he'd wake up and realize he could get someone younger and hotter and cooler than me.

I was also really confused about my sudden ability to dream about the future. According to Ed, it wasn't something that typically happened with a Genervian mate, yet it had started once we'd slept together so it couldn't be unrelated.

I couldn't figure out why this was happening, but I had a feeling if anyone could figure it out, it would be Sage Rosewater. Pepper's mother was one of the strongest and well-known witches in Colorado and was also married to a powerful psychic. She knew everything about the mystical world we lived in.

After getting someone to cover part of my shift so I could leave early, I headed over to Rosewater Emporium. The Rosewater family had been running the magic supply and bookstore for over a century. I knew that Sage usually worked at the shop on Thursdays while Cami and Stephen took their twins to some kind of parent child gymnastics class to burn off some of the kids' energy.

As soon as she saw me enter the store, Sage came out from behind the counter to give me a big hug. She was in her late fifties, with long wavy hair that was a mixture of gray and brown, and an almost ethereal figure. She had this way of looking at a person like she could see every secret in their eyes.

"Marian dear! Pepper told me that you'd found your mate. Congratulations!"

"Thanks Sage, but I actually wanted to talk to you about something, if you have a minute."

She waved her arm around the nearly empty store. "I might have to pop over to help a customer, but otherwise I'm all yours."

She pointed to two armchairs that were located across the aisle facing the cash register. "Have a seat dear. Would you like some tea?"

Before I could respond, a steaming teapot and two cups appeared on the table between the armchairs. My eyes widened. As long as I'd lived in Greysden, I still was amazed when I saw magic in action. I selected a tea bag from the dish and dunked it into my cup. Sage listened intently as I explained about my inadvertent mating with Ed and the sudden development of prophetic dreams.

"Hm, I've never seen this before." Sage looked thoughtful.

"People developing new powers?" I asked.

"Oh no, changes in power often happens when people mate, especially if their powers need a boost and their mate is a supe. That's what happened with both Cami and Meri in fact."

Sage's daughter Cami was a witch whose powers were famously glitchy. She was the sister who did a love spell to find my friend Pepper a mate and accidentally called a mate for herself. Pepper had mentioned that Cami's magic was more stable since she and Stephen had mated. And Meri's psychic skills had gotten a boost after she'd mated Preston, even though they were still hard to decipher sometimes. Kind of like my prophetic dreams.

"Then what haven't you seen before?" I asked in confusion.

"I never noticed your magic before," Sage responded. "It must have been recessive, or I would have at least seen a glimmer in your aura. I'm guessing that your mating with this alien has activated something dormant in you that's making you have these dreams."

"Are you saying I'm going to be a witch now?" I asked in confusion.

"No dear, the power I'm seeing in you now is definitely psychic power. If I had to guess, I'd bet one of your grandparents was at least half psychic."

"Seems like someone would have mentioned that," I said, immediately rejecting the idea.

My family was not the magical sort, not at all.

"Not really. In the full human world, people hide their magic to avoid persecution, or because they fear that someone will assume they are crazy. But there's definitely something different about you now. Are your parents still alive?"

"Yes, they live in Kansas."

Sage nodded like that explained a lot. "You should call them and ask if anyone in the family had premonitions or seemed a little psychic. I think you'll be surprised at the answer."

"How on Earth am I going to ask my parents if anyone in the family is psychic?" I asked. "They'll think I've lost my mind."

"Or maybe they'll be relieved that you finally know the truth."

Edfollopxen

My mate was troubled. I'd felt glimmers of nervousness and confusion coming through the mate bond all afternoon, and it got stronger as I walked over to her house.

When Marian opened the door she was talking on her communication device. She put one finger up, pointing towards the ceiling, but I wasn't sure what the gesture meant. Since she seemed to be occupied, I headed towards the kitchen to unpack our food.

Marian had introduced me to an Earth dish called "meat loaf" and when I heard it was the 'special of the day' today at the diner, I offered to pick some up for dinner. Since Marian and I both worked during the day, we took turns either cooking a simple meal or picking up food from a local restaurant.

One of my crew had mentioned that a new cooking school was opening in Greysden soon. He and his wife were signing up for a couples cooking class, and I was planning to ask Marian if she would attend with me so we could learn new skills.

I unpacked our food, setting it out on plates but leaving it covered, grabbed us both a bottle of water, then waited at the table until Marian was done with her call. When she came in, she looked upset. Her emotions felt like they were jumbled.

"Hey."

She pressed a distracted kiss on my cheek, then went to the cabinet next to the refrigerator and returned with a bottle of brown liquid and two very tiny glasses.

"What's wrong?" I asked.

She shook her head. "I need a drink first before I can talk."

She poured some of the brown liquid into each glass, sliding one towards me before lifting hers to her mouth. She seemed to toss the drink to the back of her throat, swallowing it all down in one gulp.

Following her example, I aimed the liquid towards the back of my throat and swallowed.

It felt like fire was burning the inside of my throat. I coughed, trying to expel the terrible taste. Marian watched with wide eyes, as I grabbed my water bottle and drank the entire thing down in one gulp to remove the fiery taste of the other drink. My eyes were leaking.

"Are you okay, Ed?" she asked.

I shook my head. "Yes, the fire is gone now. Well, mostly."

Marian rolled her lips in, like she was trying not to laugh at me. It was an expression I'd grown accustomed to in the short time we'd known each other. This time her efforts to contain her emotions did not work, and she started giggling. The sound was sweet and made me feel happy, even though I didn't know why she was laughing at me.

"What is funny, mate?" I growled.

My tone made her laugh more.

"Your face!" she gasped. "You should have seen your face. Your expression. It was so funny."

"I am glad you enjoyed my pain," I said with mock seriousness. "What was this poison you gave me?"

"Tequila."

At my questioning look she added, "It's a type of alcohol made from a plant called agave."

"I like beer better," I decided.

Marian walked over to the refrigerator, bringing back a bottle of beer which she handed me. I popped to top off with my fingernail – something that Marian found impressive for some reason – and she poured herself another tiny cup of tequila while I took a sip of my beer. I sighed as the cold, hoppy liquid soothed the last of the stinging from my throat.

"You really just like beer, huh?"

"I also like water, the fizzy drink in the red can, and peppermint lattes. But I must confess that beer is my favorite."

Marian smiled. I loved it when she did that.

"Shall we eat?" I suggested. "Meatloaf will make you feel better, and then you can tell me what has you feeling nervous and confused."

Marian had explained to me about how sometimes she liked to eat her feelings. After more research I'd determined that certain types of foods provided comfort to humans like Marian when they were stressed or upset.

"I don't know how I feel about this emotion detector thing you have," she said, shaking her head. "Something weird happened today, and I don't know what to make of it."

"What happened?" I put my fork down, wanting to focus on what my mate was sharing with me.

"I went to see the most powerful witches in town today. She's my friend Pepper's mother and she is an expert in the magical world. I wanted to ask her if she knew of a reason why I was suddenly having prophetic dreams."

"Did you have another one?" I asked.

"Yes. I dreamed that Bob Johnson thought his cashier had stolen money from the cash register but really, he'd dropped a stack of bills between the two sections of the counter," she said. "Then when I stopped at the market for a snack on my break, I saw Bob interrogating his employee about the money and was able to clear everything up before things got heated."

"And the witch knows why this is happening?"

She nodded. "Yeah, kind of. She says she sees psychic energy in my aura."

"You are a psychic?" I asked in surprise.

"I don't know. I guess a little bit?" Marian shrugged. "Sage thought maybe I had dormant psychic skills that were activated by our mating."

I couldn't help but puff up with satisfaction hearing that my mate mark had unlocked a new gift inside my mate. Marian rolled her eyes at my obvious pride.

"Anyway, she suggested that I call my parents to ask them if anyone in the family has any magic or psychic powers so I could get more information about what's happening to me. But when I asked them, they insisted they need to come to Greysden to talk to me in person."

"Your mother and father will be coming here?" I confirmed. "That's great! I would very much like to meet them."

Marian's expression conveyed that she did not agree with my assessment.

"It's not great, it's terrible," she asserted.

"I do not understand. I will be very happy when my parents arrive on Earth for a visit. They are eager to meet their new daughter."

I smiled as I remembered how excited my parents had been when I shared the news of my new mate with them.

"My parents are old, cranky ass bigots. They hate everyone who is different from them, and they can't forgive me for living my own life."

She studied my face for a moment. "And I'll just apologize in advance for how shitty they are going to be when they meet you."

"Surely they are happy that you have found a mate?"

"I haven't shared that bit of news with them yet."

Her face was closed off, and through the mate bond I could feel stubbornness and maybe a little bit of hurt. I couldn't understand this family dynamic that Marian was describing.

"Why have you not told them this?"

"It's none of their damned business."

Marian

Ed was clearly confused about my weird parents, and I didn't know how to explain it. He'd see for himself I guessed, because I knew there was no way he'd agree to stay away from me when my parents came this weekend.

Their insistence on coming to see me in person was startling. I'd lived in Greysden for a while now and they'd never once shown any interest in coming to visit. In fact, I hadn't seen my parents in years. Other than a brief text exchange once every couple of weeks and a phone call on Christmas, I hadn't had any in-person interaction with my parents in years.

When I called them tonight, I couldn't think of a good way to ask them about my new prophetic dreams, so I'd just blurted out my question.

***

"So, weird question, but did anyone in the family ever think they were psychic or have some kind of special powers?"

There had been a long pause before my father had asked, "Why do you ask?"

Their lack of immediate denial had made me instantly suspicious. "I've been having these really weird dreams. Then whatever I dream happens in real life."

Another long pause.

"We're coming to see you," my father said. "We'll be there on Saturday."

"What?"

My mouth dropped open in shock.

"Why would you come here?" I asked.

"We've always wanted to see your house, dear," my mother had inserted nervously.

"No, you haven't."

"We'll come on Saturday," my father said firmly. "This is best to discuss in person."

And then my damned father hung up on me.

***

I wasn't sure how long my parents intended to stay, but I had no idea how I was going to explain a town full of people who turned into animals, made pots of steaming tea appear out of thin air, or any of the other strange occurrences that happened here in Greysden.

The magical world wasn't exactly hidden, but most people – the 'normals' as Greysden's residents called us – lived blissfully unaware of what happened around them. For their part, outside of places like Greysden where everyone was accepted and able to live out in the open no matter who or what they were, the supernatural folk kept a low profile.

I wouldn't have even guessed that my parents knew about supernatural beings, but after their response to my call, I had a feeling that I was wrong about that.

Assuming my parents were going to invite themselves to stay at my place, I fixed up my guest bedroom and spent the next couple of days doing a thorough cleaning of my house. Not that it was messy, but I still was enough of my parents' daughter to want everything to look perfect when they came.

I knew Ed was concerned about my heightened emotions, and when I could separate myself from my own thoughts I could feel his confusion, but after trying to explain things to him a couple of times, I knew I just needed to let him see for himself. From his stories I could tell he came from a close knit and loving family, which was the opposite of mine.

My parents had told me that they would come on Saturday morning, but I didn't expect them to come quite as early as they did. I was still in bed, Ed's huge body wrapped around me like a cocoon and Felix sleeping on my feet when I heard the doorbell ring. Ed slept like the dead, so he barely stirred when I slipped out of bed, pulled on a robe, and went to open the door.

"Mom, Dad, what are you doing here so early?" I asked when I saw my parents on my porch. "What time is it, anyway?"

"Seven a.m.," my mother said brusquely, pushing her way past me into the house.

She took a quick look around, an expression like she'd smelled something bad on her face. My father followed us inside, but he was all business.

"Shall we talk?"

I looked at him like he was crazy.

"It's seven a.m. and I haven't even had coffee yet. When you said you were coming Saturday morning, I had no idea it would be so early."

"Why don't you come into the kitchen, and I'll put on some coffee?"

After settling my parents at the table, we made awkward small talk while I began scooping coffee grounds into the reusable filter. I heard a shrill scream behind me, making me jump and spill coffee all over the place.

"What the—? Oh, good morning, Ed."

I gave him a slightly psychotic smile. My parents had been in my house less than ten minutes and they were already driving me crazy. He strode right over to me, looking down in concern.

"My parents arrived earlier than I expected."

He nodded but didn't take his eyes off me.

"What do you need, mate?"

"I'm making coffee, then we can talk."

Ed grabbed a sponge and some paper towels, cleaning the spilled coffee grounds off the counter and the floor while I finished the coffee.

When it was finished brewing, I brought the entire pot over to the table while Ed gathered some cups.

When we sat down, I realized my parents were staring at me in horror. Felix ran up to me and jumped into my lap, cuddling against my belly as if to provide moral support. I stroked his fur, trying to keep calm.

"What's the matter?" I asked my parents. "Why are you staring at me like that?"

"Your friend is...blue."

My eyes bounced to Ed. I'd been spending so much time with him I didn't even notice the bluish tint of his skin anymore.

"No need to point it out, Mother. The man knows he's blue."

"What are you?" my father asked him with a dark frown.

"Dad!" I said sharply. "Don't be rude."

My father glowered at me. But before he could unleash whatever vitriol he was about to spill for my admonishing him, Ed interrupted.

"I am called Edfollopxen but my Earth friends call me Ed. I recently moved here from the planet of Genervia to find my mate. I have found her, she is Marian."

The room was so quiet you could hear a pin drop.

"Guess that explains the questions," my mother mumbled out of the side of her mouth.

My father nodded, looking grim.

"What is going on?" I asked impatiently.

"Don't you think he's a little young for you dear?"

My mother's voice dripped with condescension as she turned towards Ed.

"My daughter is forty-five. She is too old to have children and I can tell by the state of this house that she has no money."

I couldn't decide what to be offended by first. Fortunately, my mate came to the rescue.

"Marian is my soulmate. I do not care about the state of her reproductive organs or her financial status. I love her and will spend the rest of my life with her."

My head whipped towards the giant blue man sitting next to me.

"You love me?" I asked.

Ed's brow crinkled as he answered. "You must know this. I fell in love with you when I first saw you."

"No, you felt the mate bond when you first saw me. That's simple Genervian biology, a physical response."

He took my hand in his and met my eyes.

"I don't love you because of biology, Marian. I love you because you're kind and sweet and you buy me beer and stroke my hair when you think I'm asleep. Even if you weren't my mate, I'd still love you."

Edfollopxen

Marian's eyes looked moist but she blinked rapidly, clearing up the condition. Her mother, a harsh woman who looked like what the humans called a bird, cleared her throat, breaking the connection between us.

"We don't have all day, Marian. Let us tell you the bad news so we can get out of this god-forsaken town."

I placed my hand on Marian's thigh as I felt rage course through her.

"What bad news, Mother?"

Marian's mother dramatically pressed a hand against her bony chest.

"You tell her, Henry. It's too upsetting."

"Marian, you come from a long line of women who were mentally damaged," her father said calmly, as if he were talking about the weather.

"Damaged?" she asked incredulously.

"Yes. The women in your mother's family have a recessive gene or something, it makes them see things. It's a mental illness. Not all of them of course, thankfully your mother was spared the family curse. But unfortunately, it looks like you were not."

"What are you talking about, Dad?"

Marian's father looked towards her mother, who took a deep breath and picked up the story.

"The women in my family – not all of them, but many of them – tend to attract supernatural creatures. Genetic freaks."

She emphasized the word 'freaks', giving me a look that clearly indicated her distaste for me. I'd never anyone who'd immediately hated me before. It was disconcerting.

"As is the way with the half-breeds and misfits, they want to mate. The mating turns on some kind of psychic power that makes the women go crazy," Marian's mother explained.

"Your poor grandmother, God rest her soul, was so tortured by these nonstop psychic dreams that she became unable to tell what was real and what wasn't. She was afraid to go to sleep because she saw such terrible things in her dreams. When your grandfather died, her powers became even more unstable. We had to lock her up in an asylum until she finally passed away."

"Grandpa was a supe?" Marian asked in surprise.

"Yes, he was one quarter shifter on his mother's side. It was enough to activate your grandmother's powers though."

Marian was silent for a moment as she processed the information.

"But you don't have any powers, Mom? You don't have the dreams?"

"Fortunately, I married a purebred human – like you should do – and it kept everything latent like it should be." Her mother gave her a hard stare. "You should know, when the visions first come if there is a separation, they will wane. But the more time you spend together, the worse it will be until you completely lose your grasp on reality."

The older woman gave me another distasteful look, hostility radiating from her. I was tempted to bare my teeth and growl at her to see what she would do, but I didn't want to upset my mate.

"Now you know the truth, Marian," her father spoke up. "You've unlocked these dreams and if you stay with this, this *creature*, you will eventually go crazy. Just like your grandmother."

He pushed up from the table and took his wife's hand. "We have to go now. I hope you make the right decision, Marian, or the next time we visit you, it will be behind locked doors. We'll pray for you."

Without another word the two older humans walked out of the kitchen. The front door slammed a few seconds later.

Marian sat completely still, as if she were in shock. Her emotions were such a tumble I couldn't get a read on her.

"Mate."

She looked up at the sound of my voice, her eyes wide and glassy. She cuddled Felix against her protectively.

"Ed, I think I need to be alone."

"But we had plans today," I reminded her. "We were going to hike to top of Grey's Peak."

She shook her head. "I'm sorry. I just, I can't Ed. Please just go and let me think." Her voice turned more high-pitched. "I need to process this!"

I reached for her, intending to give her a hug, and she flinched back. From his perch on Marian's lap, Felix hissed at me as if I hadn't brought him his favorite tuna treats just last night.

"You are concerned about the story your parents told you," I guessed.

"Of course I am," she said. "It's a lot to think about."

"Do you want to talk about it?" I asked.

"No. Not right now." She was staring at her the feline reclining on her lap as if Felix held the solution to all of her problems.

"You will not go crazy mate," I tried to reassure her. "I will not let you."

"Ed, please, please just go now."

I felt a stab of pain but pushed it away. I wouldn't dream of denying a request from my mate.

"Can I come back tonight?" I asked. "I will bring pizza."

Pizza was my mate's favorite food.

"No," she avoided my gaze. "I...I'll let you know when I'm ready to hang out again. Please don't come again until I'm ready to see you."

We hadn't slept apart in weeks. I was at a loss for what to do. I'd never seen Marian like this. So distant. Her internal light dimmed. I knew I should help her, but the only thing I could think to do was to comply with her request, as much as I hated it.

"I will go," I said, wincing when I saw the relief in her eyes. "But remember what I told you, mate. I love you. I love you as you are right now, and I will love you as you will be in the future. Nothing will change that."

Leaning down, I pressed my lips briefly to the top of her head. "Contact me when you are ready to see me again."

She didn't answer.

Marian

It would not be an understatement to say that the last month had been crazy. First a big blue alien came into the library on April Fool's Day and said I was his mate. Then after giving me some mind blowing orgasms, he'd connected us with an unbreakable mating bond.

I'd tried to stay away from him, but eventually the pull was too strong. And the truth was, I liked Ed. I liked falling asleep in his arms and waking up with him wrapped around me. I liked hanging out with him. I liked introducing him to Earth culture. I liked him a lot.

You more than like him, I told myself. As unlikely as our relationship was, I'd fallen for Ed. But that didn't solve the 'me going insane' problem.

I wanted to pretend like the story my parents had told me was bullshit, but as they'd spoken, I remembered whispers of things I'd heard as a kid. Things that didn't make sense back then, but totally made sense now, like people whispering about my 'crazy' grandmother.

I could understand why the dreams would make someone lose their mind. I woke up each morning totally uncertain which dreams were premonitions and which dreams were just dreams. Waiting around for things to happen like they did in my dreams was exhausting.

After spending the rest of the weekend fretting – and missing my mate – I decided another visit with Sage Rosewater was in order. When Pepper told her mom I was trying to get in touch with her, Sage invited me to the Rosewater Mansion for dinner.

Pepper's family owned a giant estate with a huge Victorian mansion and acres of woods that backed up against the public woods in Greysden. The place was filled with antiques and magical paraphernalia, yet it was clean and welcoming.

"Thank you for having me, Sage," I said politely. "I appreciate you taking the time to talk to me."

"It's no problem, dear," Sage said. "My husband is playing poker tonight and Pepper is out helping Meri with an event, so I'm glad to have some company."

My friend Pepper still lived with her parents, but their mansion was large enough that she had her own suite on the opposite side of the house from her parents. She'd told me many times that sometimes she could go days without seeing her parents.

Over a meal of roasted chicken and potatoes I told Sage about the weird visit from my parents and all that they'd said.

"The strange thing is, I think they were right. I haven't had one psychic dream since Ed left my house Saturday."

Sage stared at me for so long I started to squirm. "What?"

"I was just wondering why a person who could have dreams that can help people would deliberately try to avoid them," Sage said. "Would you rather that little pup you saved have gotten hit by a car?"

"Of course not!"

"Yet you have no idea what messages the universe is trying to send through you this week while you've been separated from Ed and unable to receive the visions."

"I don't want to go crazy," I said stubbornly. "My grandmother had to be locked up!"

"I suspect your grandmother had to be locked up because she was anguished missing her mate, not because of her visions. But even if that was the reason, you forgot Marian, you live here in Greysden. There are any number of us who can help you manage the dreams, or at least to figure out which ones are regular dreams and which ones are psychic messages."

"You can do that?" I asked in surprise.

"Of course. You just need to learn to train your mind to differentiate between them with a few sessions of lucid dreaming. It'll be a piece of cake. Speaking of cake..."

She snapped her fingers and two large slices of German chocolate cake appeared on the table. "Let's have dessert and then we'll get started."

I went over to train with Sage Rosewater for the next few days, and even without having Ed near me, she was able to use her power to jumpstart my visions again. By the end of the week, I was confidently able to distinguish between regular dreams and visions. Once I got the hang of it, it was surprisingly easy.

The only thing that wasn't easy was being away from my mate. I'd purposely kept my distance from Ed so I wouldn't get distracted while I tried to figure out how to harness my new powers, but every day we were apart I felt worse. His absence was a physical ache, and more than that, I missed him.

On the one hand, I appreciated that he'd respected my wishes to wait for me to tell him when we should see each other again. On the other hand, I was disappointed that he didn't at least try to get into contact with me.

I know, I was a hypocrite. But I couldn't help but wonder, had he moved on already? Found another woman to be his mate? He might have even left Earth for all I knew, because I'd been unable to pick up anything through our mate bond since he left. That had to mean something, right?

By Friday I couldn't take it anymore. I had to see Ed. I needed to apologize to him for shutting him out. And I needed to feel those strong blue arms wrapped around me again.

Realizing that I didn't actually know how to communicate with Ed with the mate bond not functioning, I resolved to figure out where he was staying. I remembered him mentioning that he'd moved his ship close to a large lake on the north side of Greysden, so I got up early on Saturday morning, put on my hiking shoes, and set out to find my mate.

An hour later I was tired, sweating, and lost.

"Damn it, Ed!" I yelled up at the trees. "Why can't you have a cell phone like a normal person? How is it that we live in the same small town and haven't seen each other all week? I swear to God if you've abandoned me, I'm going track you down and kick your big blue ass!"

"Why would I abandon you? You are my mate."

I jumped as I heard Ed's voice behind me. Whirling around, I pressed my palm against my racing heart.

"Jeez, don't sneak up on people like that!" I groused.

"I am sorry, you were yelling and couldn't hear me approach."

I eyed Ed hungrily. He was wearing shiny looking pants and a shirt that was open, revealing the planes of his strong chest.

"Why are you dressed like that?" I asked suspiciously. "Were you going back to Genervia? Were you with another woman?"

He strode towards me with a determined look on his face, large hands coming to cup my shoulders. The minute he touched me, everything inside me calmed.

"I am not going anywhere or doing anything without you, mate. I have struggled to sleep without you by my side, and I was still in bed when I heard you thrashing about in the forest. I threw on the first items of clothing that I could find. I'm sorry they are not pleasing to you."

I looked up at his handsome blue face. "Are you mad at me, Ed? I'm so sorry for pushing you away, but I needed some space. What my parents told me, it was a lot to process."

"I am not angry with you, mate," he reassured me.

"Okay well, I'm angry with you then. How dare you ditch me?"

"Ditch? Is this not a trench in the ground?"

I sighed. "Ditch means abandon. I haven't seen you all week!"

His brow creased in confusion. "I did exactly as you asked me. I went away and waited for you to let me know you were ready."

I knew I wasn't being fair to him, but I couldn't help it.

"Then why couldn't I feel anything through the mate bond?"

"Ah. Yes. I blocked it. That is why."

I smacked his chest as hard as I could. It was like hitting a concrete wall.

"Don't do that again unless we both agree!"

One corner of his mouth quirked up and his eyes started dancing, like he was trying not to laugh.

"Don't you laugh at me, mate! I was worried sick when I couldn't feel you! I thought you left Earth or something."

A huge smile split his face. "You called me mate!"

"Yeah, so?"

Instead of answering me, Ed picked me up by the waist and flung me over his shoulder. One arm banded across my legs to hold me in place as he started running through the forest.

"What are you doing?" I cried.

"Bringing you to my ship so I can mate with you until you are unable to forget who you belong to."

Edfollopxen

My mate was a strong and independent female and I'd consciously avoided acting too possessive around her, nervous that I might scare her off. But our long separation followed by finding her frantically looking for me in the woods had severely frayed my self-control.

Hearing Marian call me 'mate' had severed it.

When I scented my mate's arousal at my possessive language, I knew she liked it. It made me run faster. As soon as my ship came into sight, I gave the order to open the door, bringing her inside and closing the door behind us.

I set Marian on her feet and before she could do so much as take a breath, I literally ripped her shirt off her body.

"Hey! I like that shirt," she protested.

I ignored her, making quick work of shredding the confining materials that covered her beautiful breasts. She shoved her pants down before I could touch them, but I couldn't resist ripping her silky panties off her body. She moaned and the cabin of my ship filled with the sweet scent of her arousal.

Undressing quickly, I picked her up again and tossed her on the bed. Intended for solo travel, it was narrow and too small for two people, but I climbed up on top of her, pinning her between me and the mattress.

I lowered my head and gave her a claiming kiss, only pulling apart when we were both breathless. Slowly I kissed and nipped my way down her neck and across her shoulders until I reached her full breasts. They jiggled a bit with every heaving breath she took.

Rolling one nipple between my fingers, I lowered my head to suckle the other. I teased the top with my tongue until she started wiggling beneath me, then I bit down hard. She gasped in pleasure.

I was determined to remind her that I was her mate, and that no one else could please her as I could. I kissed along her ribs and down to the soft pillow of her belly. I knew she was most self-conscious of this area, wishing it were flat instead of having the little pooch that she despised. I showed her with my lips and hands how much I loved it before finally making my way to her pussy.

Oral sex wasn't something I knew about before I met Marian but since I'd learned about this way to pleasure a woman, I'd done much research on how to develop skills in this area.

When I teased and tapped against Marian's clit, I knew I was on the right track. I slipped my fingers between the lips of her *afghaxoya,* then pressed one finger against her entrance until she practically sucked me in. Meanwhile the vibrating sound my body made was getting stronger and louder.

"Holy fuck," she gasped right before she came apart beneath me, her legs tightening against my head and moving restlessly.

When I looked up at her, my lips and chin were dripping with her arousal.

She raised her head and gave me a suspicious look. "How have you gotten even better at that since we've been apart?"

"I've been researching techniques." Her eyes narrowed and I hastened to add, "On your internet."

I slid back up her body, covering her with my bulk. With one elbow on the side of her head to brace me and keep some of my weight off her chest, I cuffed my hand around her neck lightly, just enough to assert control.

"You are mine and I am yours, mate. There is no other *afghaxoya* I will be licking or fucking in this lifetime."

"You have a unique ability to make something sound both filthy and sweet," she mused.

"I am glad I amuse you," I said, levering off the bed. "Now get on your hands and knees so I can claim you."

She rolled her eyes but complied. Once she was settled in place, I moved behind her, wasting no time in lining up my *afgha* with her opening. Holding her hips in place, I pushed inside her in one long shove, everything inside me finally calming down for the first time in a week as her inner muscles squeezed me tight.

Marian had her hair tied up with an elastic band, giving me the perfect opportunity to wrap her ponytail around my fist and use it to arch her neck so I could kiss her. While our tongues tangled I began to move, wasting no time with going slow. I was too far gone for slow.

When Marian moaned, I released her lips and moved my hands back to her hips. With a low growl, I began rutting into her like an animal, never slowing even when her inner muscles squeezed and my mate shuddered through her second orgasm. I had a desperate urge to mark her inside and out and I couldn't rest until I felt my seed leaving my body, painting her womb with every hard thrust of my hips.

As I emptied myself inside her, my teeth caught the scar on her shoulder, nipping the spot to reinforce my claim on her.

My orgasm went on and on until I worried that I'd pass out before I finished. When I finally relaxed against her and slid out of her body, a long stream of my cum dripped down her legs. The sight gave me primal satisfaction.

I shifted, lifting Marian in the air with my arms, then pulling her on top of my body after I laid down on my back on the bunk. She snuggled against me, sleepy and sated.

"That was something," she mumbled sleepily.

"Something wonderful," I agreed. I wrapped my arms around her, and we both fell asleep.

When we woke again it was midday, the sun shining through the clear ceiling of my ship. Marian looked around curiously.

"Your ship is so small," she said. "It's hardly bigger than my closet. I can't believe you spent six months in this thing."

"The sacrifice was worth it," I told her earnestly. "It brought me to my mate and helped me find love."

Marian looked down at me. "I love you, Ed. I'm ready now. If you still want me, I'm all-in with the mate thing."

"That is good," I told her with a big smile. "Because you cannot push me away any longer."

"There's just one thing," she said.

"What is it?" I asked.

"You're going to need to move into my place. I need my closet space. Plus, Felix would not like being confined like this."

I cupped her face in my hands and brought her lips down close to mine. "Now that you have said you love me and have acknowledged our mating, I will live with you anywhere you want."

"Me and Felix, you mean?"

I paused, thinking of the jealous feline. "Yes, as long as there's also beer."

Epilogue – Marian

Six months later...

"I hope your parents will like me."

I wrung my hands nervously, surprised at how important it was to me that my mate's parents accepted me. Ed had repeatedly assured me that his people were very accepting of their people mating with other species, but I couldn't forget the look on my own parents' faces when they saw Ed in my kitchen that morning they visited.

Ed and I had been living together for six months and I'd never been happier. Every day I went to my job at the library, and he went to his job at Grey Construction. After work we'd make dinner together, grab carryout, or meet friends for dinner. Felix and Ed had even made a tentative peace.

My friend Pepper finally found her mate and the four of us went out often. Ed was also pretty tight with his boss Stuart Grey and some of the other wolf shifters he worked with, so we saw them socially as well.

In his spare time Ed was teaching himself to brew beer, and he was very excited to debut one of his new brews when his parents arrived.

Right on time, we heard a knock on the door. An extremely handsome silver fox – or maybe it was a blue fox? – was on my front porch. Tall and broad with white hair and sparkling eyes, I would have recognized the man as Ed's father anywhere. Next to him was an elegant looking woman with white hair and a form-fitting shiny white dress that sparkled against her blue skin.

Ed's mother rushed forward, pulling first Ed and then me into a tight hug. She was a good hugger, and I immediately felt at ease with her.

"Marian!" Ed's mom had a soft and cultured sounding voice. "We welcome you to our family and we're so glad you are able to put up with our son."

It took me a second to realize she was teasing me, but then we all laughed, breaking the last of the tension of meeting someone new.

We all looked down as Felix meowed insistently. I picked him up and hugged him to my chest. "This is my cat, Felix."

Ed's mother scored big points with me when she reached her hand out to pet my feline companion. When Ed tried to do the same, Felix jumped out of my arms and flounced away. So much for that tentative peace.

"Mother, Father," Ed said. "I will show you to your bed chambers and then I will introduce you to the best Earth delicacy: bacon cheeseburgers. I know you must be hungry from your long trip."

While Ed's parents freshened up in the guest room, we worked together to gather items for the barbecue. Some of Ed's work friends had taught him the fine art of grilling, so we'd purchased a nice sized propane grill. Ed cooked outside every chance we got, the taste of seared meat more to his liking than that cooked indoors. As I watched him fill up the grill with a variety of meat and vegetables, I felt my heart swell with happiness.

"What are you thinking about, mate?" Ed's eyes turned towards mine. "I am feeling very happy feelings coming through the mate bond."

I moved closer, wrapping my arm around his waist.

"I was just thinking about how I thought I was content with my life, but I didn't know what I was missing until you wandered into my library."

"It was the best day of my life," he said solemnly.

Leaning up, I pressed a quick kiss to his blue jaw.

"I'm so happy you found me, Ed. I love you so much."

"I love you too, mate. Now let's grill this cow so we can eat and drink beer."

***

You can read more stories about the residents of Greysden, including the Rosewaters and the town's shifters, by visiting books2read.com/rl/Greysden[1]

**** If you liked this book, please leave a review ****

*

Keep reading for a special except from "Wolf Doctor[2]", book one of the fan-favorite "Bite-Sized Shifters" paranormal romantic comedy series.

---

1. https://books2read.com/rl/Greysden

2. https://books2read.com/u/4AOXXK

Special Preview

Wolf Doctor: A Paranormal Romantic Comedy

Twilight. Colt's favorite time of the day.

Stripping off his clothes, he took a deep breath, inhaling the scents in the air. He broke into a run and felt his body change mid-stride. In less than thirty seconds he had transformed from man to wolf.

Muscles and bone lengthening as gray hair sprouted all over his body, almost white in some places. His sharp canine teeth extended from his thickening jaw. He felt his tail grow behind him and he wagged it happily from side to side as he increased his pace, moving so fast his paws seemed to barely touch the ground.

Colt's senses were immediately heightened. His vision was sharper, his ears taking in even the softest sound, and his nose twitched with the wonderful scents of the pristine forest.

He headed through the woods, exhilarating in the feeling of free movement. His wolf loved to run. He hadn't shifted in almost a week. Too long. He needed this. He needed to shift and let his wolf run as much as he needed oxygen or food.

Speaking of food, he could use a snack. He scented a group of hares a mile away and headed in that direction at a gallop. His paws ate up the ground as he tracked the smaller beasts, stopping occasionally to sniff the ground and pick up their trail.

There, up ahead, he saw a flash of fur. He moved quickly, ears pinned back, as his wolf took over, the ultimate predator.

He could smell the fear on the hare as it took off, running for its life. Colt pulled his gums back in a canine smile. He loved the chase. The harder the capture, the better it tasted.

He sped up, following the hare instinctively as it took a sharp turn to the side. He pounced, leaping after the hare. Suddenly his feet hit air. And then he was falling. Fast.

Oh crap. He had overshot and gone right over the edge of the bluff. He could practically feel the stupid hare laughing at him as he tumbled down the embankment, scrambling but unable to stop his downward momentum.

He whined as his body hit the road below with a heavy thump.

Before he could recover he heard the squealing of brakes and suddenly he was airborne again. He landed on the asphalt a second time, feeling bones breaking and muscles tearing. He smelled the scent of his own blood and dimly heard voices as he struggled to stay conscious.

"Oh my god Dennis, you hit that poor dog!" The woman sounded upset.

"I'm not sure that it's a dog Sandy, it might be a wolf," someone, presumably Dennis, responded.

Not a dog, his wolf snipped in his head, clearly offended.

Really, that's your top worry right now? he asked his wolf.

Like all shifters, Colt shared space in his mind with his animal. He and his wolf shared not only the same body, but also the same consciousness.

He noted dimly that the humans who had hit him had exited their truck and were watching him cautiously from where they had stopped. He thought about getting up and whined again. The pain was terrible. It was impossible to move.

"He's bleeding and he's in pain," Sandy said, her voice sounding closer. "We have to get him to the animal hospital."

"There's no way he's going to survive," Dennis answered. "Let me get my shotgun out of the truck and I'll put the poor thing out of his misery."

Colt lifted his head in alarm, although it cost him dearly. He made eye contact with the woman, trying to communicate with her. He tried to make himself look sad and unthreatening. He did not want to die on the side of the road, and he definitely did not want to be put down by some random human with a shotgun. With his luck the guy would be a bad shot and make his injuries even worse.

"NO," Sandy said firmly. "You are not shooting him Dennis. Get the tarp. We'll put him in the back and drive him to the vet."

"He's a wounded animal Sandy," Dennis argued. "He may attack us, especially if he is a wolf."

Sandy continued to hold Colt's gaze. "No, he won't," she replied. "Come on, let's get him some help."

Colt passed out, not knowing who would win their argument. He just hoped it was Sandy.

He did not feel the couple cautiously wrapping him in a tarp and dragging him up into the back of their pick-up. He didn't feel himself sliding around in the truck bed as they raced to the animal hospital. He didn't hear the people loading him onto a gurney and wheeling his large body into the hospital. Both his body and his mind were completely shut down now, blissfully blocking the pain.

Then he felt it. A jolt of happiness and peace.

He opened his eyes, staring through the pain as an angel looked down at him. The overhead light glowed behind her like a halo. Thick brown hair framed her beautiful face. Her eyes were deep brown and impossibly kind.

"What happened?" his angel asked. Her voice made him feel calm. She seemed familiar.

"I think he took a header off a cliff. I think he came rolling down from up above. Suddenly there he was, falling onto the road right in front of us," Dennis explained. "Before I could stop, I hit him with my truck. I didn't do it on purpose, he seemed to come out of nowhere."

The angel's hand dropped gently to his head, rubbing him softly between his ears. He closed his eyes again, pressing against the warmth of her hand and whining softly. He had one thought before he passed out again. *Mate!*

***

For more of Colt and Valerie's story, check out "Wolf Doctor" by Rose Bak. Available now for download[1] at all major online retailers. Binge the whole series today.

---

1. *https://books2read.com/u/4AOXXK*

Other Books by Rose Bak

Magical Midlife Series
Beltane Magic (prequel)
Love Potion
Psychic Flashes
Halloween Surprise
Giant Love
Kitchen Magic
Alien Feeling

Bite-Sized Shifters Paranormal Romance Series
Long Distance Wolf
Wolf Doctor
Kat's Dog
Designer Wolf
Wolf Sheriff
Cocktail Wolf
Second Chance Wolf
Runaway Wolf

Holidays with the Shifters Series
Santa's Claws
Bear Humbug
Jingle Bear
Silver Paws
Joy to the Wolf
Lion's Heart

Boozy Book Club Series
Beach Reads
Bubbly & Billionaires
Martinis & Mysteries
Bourbon & Bikers
Midlife Madness

Extra Innings
The Proposal Solution

The Silver Fox Falls Series
Unexpected Gift
Unexpected Love
Unexpected Life

The Good with Numbers Holiday Romance Series
Love Unmasked
The Thanksgiving Scrooge
Maid for Christmas
Countdown to Love
Valentine's Lottery
Christmas Angel

Loving the Holidays Contemporary Romance Series
Dating Santa
New Year's Steve
Independence Dave
Comfort & Joy
Faking It with the Detective
Dropping the Ball
Island Getaway

Midlife Crisis Contemporary Romance Series
Summer Wedding
Roasting with Rob
Christmas Punch
Disaster Planning
Saving Texas
Texas Christmas
Factory Reset
Canadian Doctor
Second Chance to Score
Tempted at Midnight

Silver Fox Falls Midlife Romance
Unexpected Gift
Unexpected Love
Unexpected Life
The Oliver Boys Band Contemporary Romance Series
Until You Came Along
Rock Star Teacher
Rock Star Writer
Rock Star Neighbor
Rock Star Lawyer
The Diamond Bay Contemporary Romance Series
Brand New Penny
Fresh as a Daisy
Right as Rain
Reunited Series
Together Again
Finding My Baby
King of the Reunion
Caught by My Best Friend
Standalones
Beach Wedding
Jessie's Girl
Non-fiction
What to Do If You Find a Cougar in Your Living Room: Self-Care in an Uncaring World
It's All About Relationships: Reflections on Love, Friendship, and Connection

Catch up with these and other stories coming soon. Join my newsletter for more information[1] or follow my author page on your favorite retailer.

---

1. *https://storyoriginapp.com/giveaways/62ee758e-068f-11eb-904e-c373f6014fe1*

About the Author

Rose Bak has been obsessed with books since she got her first library card at age five. She is a passionate reader with an e-reader bursting with thousands of beloved books.

Although Rose enjoys writing both fiction and nonfiction, romance novels have always been her favorite guilty pleasure, both as a reader and an author. Rose's contemporary romance books focus on strong female characters over thirty-five and the alpha males who love them. Expect a lot of steam, a little bit of snark, and a guaranteed happily ever after.

Rose lives in the Pacific Northwest with her family, and special needs dogs. In addition to writing, she also teaches accessible yoga and loves music. Sadly, she has absolutely no musical talent, so she mostly sings in the shower.

Please sign up for the Rose Bak Romance newsletter[1] to get a free book and keep up to date on all the latest news. You can also follow Rose on Facebook[2], Instagram[3], Twitter[4], Goodreads[5], or Bookbub[6].

---

1. https://storyoriginapp.com/giveaways/62ee758e-068f-11eb-904e-c373f6014fe1

2. https://www.facebook.com/AuthorRoseBak

3. https://www.instagram.com/authorrosebak/

4. https://twitter.com/AuthorRoseBak

5. https://www.goodreads.com/authorrosebak

6. https://www.bookbub.com/authors/rose-bak

Don't miss out!

Visit the website below and you can sign up to receive emails whenever Rose Bak publishes a new book. There's no charge and no obligation.

https://books2read.com/r/B-A-VATM-ZVETC

BOOKS 2 READ

Connecting independent readers to independent writers.

www.ingramcontent.com/pod-product-compliance
Lightning Source LLC
Chambersburg PA
CBHW031425130726
47989CB00003B/1031